"That's Gwen Murphy standing there, *Jess reminded himself.* **She'd rather slug a man than kiss him.**

But with her hair all sleep mussed and her curves in that old cotton robe that showed more leg than he guessed she was aware of, she looked sexier than any woman in the flimsiest negligee.

"You're still here," Gwen grumbled.

"I told you I'd see you through your recent loss."

"Not necessary," Gwen replied. But, suddenly light-headed, she slumped against the doorjamb.

Jess reached her and lifted her into his arms. Her robe opened more, and he realized she was wearing little or nothing under it. Arousal threatened again.

Gwen yanked her robe around her and rasped, "Put me down."

He must be crazy to be attracted to her, Jess thought. He liked his women soft and sweet.

While tangling with Gwen…would be like tangling with a cougar!

Dear Reader,

Spring cleaning wearing you out? Perk up with a heart-thumping romance from Silhouette Romance. This month, your favorite authors return to the line, and a new one makes her debut!

Take a much-deserved break with bestselling author Judy Christenberry's secret-baby story, *Daddy on the Doorstep* (#1654). Then plunge into Elizabeth August's latest, *The Rancher's Hand-Picked Bride* (#1656), about a celibate heroine forced to find her rugged neighbor a bride!

You won't want to miss the first in Raye Morgan's CATCHING THE CROWN miniseries about three royal siblings raised in America who must return to their kingdom and marry. In *Jack and the Princess* (#1655), Princess Karina falls for her bodyguard, but what will it take for this gruff commoner to win a place in the royal family? And in Diane Pershing's *The Wish* (#1657), the next SOULMATES installment, a pair of magic eyeglasses gives Gerri Conklin the chance to do over the most disastrous week of her life…and find the man of her dreams!

And be sure to keep your eye on these two Romance authors. Roxann Delaney delivers her third fabulous Silhouette Romance novel, *A Whole New Man* (#1658), about a live-for-the-moment hero transformed into a family man, but will it last? And Cheryl Kushner makes her debut with *He's Still the One* (#1659), a fresh, funny, heartwarming tale about a TV show host who returns to her hometown and the man she never stopped loving.

Happy reading!

Mary-Theresa Hussey

Mary-Theresa Hussey
Senior Editor

Please address questions and book requests to:
Silhouette Reader Service
U.S.: 3010 Walden Ave., P.O. Box 1325, Buffalo, NY 14269
Canadian: P.O. Box 609, Fort Erie, Ont. L2A 5X3

The Rancher's Hand-Picked Bride

ELIZABETH AUGUST

SILHOUETTE Romance

Published by Silhouette Books

America's Publisher of Contemporary Romance

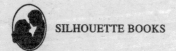 **SILHOUETTE BOOKS**

ISBN 0-373-19656-3

THE RANCHER'S HAND-PICKED BRIDE

Books by Elizabeth August

Silhouette Romance

Author's Choice #554
Truck Driving Woman #590
Wild Horse Canyon #626
Something So Right #668
The Nesting Instinct #719
Joey's Father #749
Ready-Made Family #771
The Man from Natchez #790
A Small Favor #809
The Cowboy and the Chauffeur #833
Like Father, Like Son #857
The Wife He Wanted #881
*The Virgin Wife #921
*Haunted Husband #922
*Lucky Penny #945
*A Wedding for Emily #953

*The Seeker #989
†The Forgotten Husband #1019
†Ideal Dad #1054
†A Husband for Sarah #1067
The Bridal Shower #1091
*A Father's Vow #1126
*A Handy Man To Have Around #1157
The Rancher and the Baby #1187
*The Determined Virgin #1229
Paternal Instincts #1265
The Bride's Second Thought #1288
Marrying O'Malley #1386
Truly, Madly, Deeply #1404
A Royal Mission #1446
Slade's Secret Son #1512
The Rancher's Hand-Picked Bride #1656

Silhouette Special Edition

One Last Fling! #871
*The Husband #1059

Silhouette Intimate Moments

Girls' Night Out #880
Logan's Bride #950

Silhouette Books

Jingle Bells, Wedding Bells 1994
"The Forever Gift"

36 Hours
Cinderella Story

*Smytheshire, Massachusetts
†Where the Heart Is

ELIZABETH AUGUST

lives in western North Carolina with her husband, Doug. They have three grown sons. She began writing romances soon after their youngest was born.

After a bout with cancer, she has learned to relax and enjoy life more. To this end, she has taken up golf. She says her game could use a great deal of improvement, but the beauty of the mountain courses takes her mind off of her bad shots.

Elizabeth has published under the pseudonym of Betsy Page for Harlequin.

Chapter One

Gwendolen Murphy, known to friends and foes alike as Gwen, grimaced distastefully as she turned onto Logan property. It had taken her nearly an hour to get here from Lubbock and the ranch house was another half a mile from the main road. The Texas heat was oppressive and halfway there her air-conditioning had decided not to work. Her short chestnut hair was damp with perspiration and beginning to curl into little ringlets, the back of her shirt where it rested against the seat was wet and her jeans were clinging with an uncomfortable heaviness. But the physical discomfort wasn't what was gnawing at her.

Coming back to this small bit of Texas brought too many unhappy memories. The tiny frame house she and her mother had lived in was on property that abutted the Logan ranch. Just driving past the place where she'd spent her childhood had sent a cold chill down Gwen's spine. Memories of her two stepfathers interspersed between her mother's boyfriends, the smell of liquor in the house all of the time, her mother passed out on the couch, had assailed her. Her mother hadn't been a bad woman, just a weak one. Something Gwen had vowed never to be.

And then there was Jess Logan. Since grade school, she and Jess had harbored a mutual dislike. It was, she knew, more her doing than his. Even at that young age, her reaction to him had been defensive. He'd stirred emotions within her that made her uneasy, and the distrust of men she'd learned from watching her mother had fed that uneasiness. As a result, she'd rejected his initial offer of friendship and from then on both had avoided each other whenever possible. Still, the uneasy effect he had on her had been constantly there, deep inside, a nagging something she'd worked hard to kill. When she'd moved to Lubbock following her mother's death, she'd figured he was one thorn that was out of her life for good.

"I don't know why I agreed to come," she grumbled. But that wasn't true. She'd come because Morning Hawk, Jess's great-grandmother, had summoned her. There were those who thought the old woman was a few bales short of a full load. Others were intimidated by her. And they all had good reason. Morning Hawk could be enigmatic and cantankerous, but Gwen owed her. It was a debt that dated back to Gwen's early teens...and was the only time, until today, that Gwen had ever had any contact with Morning Hawk.

Parking in front of the ranch house, she saw the elderly, pure-blooded Apache, small, bent and looking withered with age, sitting in a rocking chair on the porch. As Gwen left the car and mounted the short flight of steps, Morning Hawk rose to greet her.

"I have a quest for you," the woman said without any preamble.

Gwen felt as if she'd stepped back in time about a hundred years. "A quest?"

Morning Hawk motioned for Gwen to follow her into the house. It was a large, well-maintained home, furnished comfortably. More upscale than most ranch houses, but then the Logans could afford it. Oil had been struck on their land several years earlier. But in spite of the enormous added income the find had produced, it was still a working ranch. Jess's father had died years earlier. His two brothers had followed in their father's footsteps and become Texas Rangers. Jess had been the one who had stayed home to run the ranch for his mother. Gwen hoped he was out on the range and would stay there until she was gone.

"Come along." Morning Hawk took her by the arm and guided her down a hallway. Stopping in front of a closed door, Morning Hawk knocked sharply, then opened the door and, with Gwen still in tow, entered.

Seated at the desk in the study punching buttons on a computer keyboard was Jess Logan. Half-Apache, his Native American heritage was strong in his rugged features. His muscular build and callused hands gave evidence that a great deal of his time was spent in manual labor. Gwen had to fight down the urge to turn and run. Silently she cursed herself. In spite of all the effort she'd put into trying to rid herself of this effect he had on her, it was as strong as ever.

Jess frowned at his great-grandmother. "You said you had someone coming this morning it was important I meet with."

His tone told Gwen she didn't fall into that category.

Well, he wasn't on her list of people she wanted to see either.

"Remember your manners," Morning Hawk admonished. She motioned for the two of them to be seated as she seated herself.

Neither obeyed.

"I don't believe there is anything Miss Murphy and I have to discuss." Jess headed to the door, adding over his shoulder, "I've got work to do."

"Jess Logan, you will sit down," Morning Hawk commanded. "And listen to what I have to say."

Outwardly, Gwen kept her expression blank. Inwardly, she couldn't help but smile at the way this order from such a tiny old shriveled woman stopped the mountain of a cowboy in his tracks.

"All right, I'll give you five minutes," he grumbled, taking his seat behind the desk.

Her curiosity overcoming her discomfort in Jess's presence, Gwen seated herself without protest. Morning Hawk knew of the animosity between Gwen and her grandson. Everyone did. They just didn't know why it existed. Even Jess, Gwen knew, had been stunned by the intensity with which she'd rejected his offer of friendship. But Gwen wasn't willing to reveal to anyone how much she feared the very womanly sensations his presence evoked. She didn't even like admitting them to herself. In the end, people, Jess included, had decided that it was one of those chemistry things—like oil and water or opposite poles of a magnet that repelled each other. So why would the elderly Apache insist on having the two of them in the same room together?

Morning Hawk turned her full attention to Gwen. "I understand you run a very personalized investigative service. You are hired by people who aren't certain they can trust the man or woman they are dating and want to know the whole truth about them?''

Her intonation made her words a question and Gwen elaborated on the service she provided. ''In today's world, people move around a great deal. That makes it easy for a person to change their past to suit their present needs. And then there's the Internet. Someone from New York might meet a person from Alaska online and begin a long-distance romance, but how does either one know the other is telling the truth? They don't. So one or the other hires me to find out.''

Morning Hawk nodded approvingly as if to say what she had just been told was what she had wanted to hear. ''So in a way you are a matchmaker.''

''More of a match breaker, usually,'' Gwen corrected. ''You would be amazed by the lies people will tell to deceive others.''

''No. No, I would not. And that brings me to the reason I arranged this meeting.'' Morning Hawk turned her attention to Jess. ''It is time you took a wife.''

Jess shook his head. ''I knew you were up to something when you started humming as soon as Mom and Grandma left for California to visit Uncle Crow. I'll get married when I'm good and ready. And right now, I'm just not ready to take that step.''

''You're twenty-nine, that's old enough to be good and ready,'' Morning Hawk returned.

Jess frowned. ''Why this sudden interest in my marital status? Both of my brothers were older than I am now when they got married.''

''I'm getting on in years. I want to see you happily settled before I pass on.'' Morning Hawk returned her attention to Gwen. "And that's where you come in. I want you to find him a wife."

Gwen's eyes rounded in shock while her stomach knotted tightly. "You want *me* to find *him* a wife?"

Jess's frown darkened until it reminded Gwen of thunderclouds gathering the sky. "I'll find my own wife."

"You're too busy running this ranch for your mother and overseeing the family's oil interests. And," Morning Hawk added sharply, "I didn't care at all for that last floozy you were seeing. She made me question your taste or, at least, the places where you meet women."

"Floozy?" Jess questioned pointedly. "Are you talking about Jeanette Harrison, our neighbor's daughter? She speaks four languages. She's traveled all over the world and she has a personal fortune of her own. I don't believe *floozy* is a fair description."

"Well, she'd never be happy living here. That socialite mother of hers has made certain that no Texas dust settled on her daughter. You need a woman who will love this land and this kind of life as much as you do."

Jess's gaze leveled on his great-grandmother. "I will choose the kind of woman I want to marry."

Morning Hawk stared back at him. "I can be just as hardheaded as you."

"More," he muttered under his breath.

"This is important to me. I rarely ask you to do something for me, but I'm asking now. Let Gwen find three women who fit both your criteria and mine. Take them out. Get to know them. If none of them appeals to you, I will feel that I have, at least, done my best."

For a long moment Jess made no response. Then in

an easy drawl, he said, "I want your word that if I do this, you will never interfere in my private life again."

"You have my word."

Gwen had watched from the sidelines with dry amusement. She knew Morning Hawk's reputation for getting what she wanted, but she also knew how stubborn Jess could be and had no doubt he would win out. Suddenly realizing that he was conceding to his great-grandmother's wishes, her amusement vanished. "Now, wait. Wait just one minute," she blurted. "Finding a wife is a lot more difficult than investigating someone. I really don't think I'm the person for this job."

Morning Hawk smiled at her. "Of course you are. I trust you. You're a good, decent person and I know you will do an excellent job."

Jess smiled cynically. "What Gwen means is that she doesn't think she can find a woman who'd put up with me."

Morning Hawk's gaze swung back to him. "Considering the way you behave sometimes, I can't blame her. But I know you better than she does. You'll make a fine husband...provided she finds a woman who knows how to handle you."

"I really can't take this job," Gwen insisted, rising from her chair.

Morning Hawk rose, too, and laid a hand on Gwen's arm. "But you must. You're the only one I would trust with such a quest. Even though you and my great-grandson obviously have a strong personality clash that has prevented you from being friends, you're an honest person who would do her best, no matter what the circumstances."

"I'm not a matchmaker."

"Let me talk to Gwen alone," Jess interjected.

"It won't do any good." Gwen edged toward the door. She was uncomfortable being in the same room with Jess Logan. The last thing she wanted was to be alone in one with him.

Challenge showed in Jess's eyes. "Don't tell me you're afraid...not the leather-tough lady who can handle every problem on her own."

Gwen's shoulders straightened with defiance. "Don't be ridiculous. Of course I'm not afraid of you."

"Behave yourselves," Morning Hawk ordered, heading to the door.

Gwen barely heard, her gaze locked with Jess's, blocking out nearly everything else. When Jess was angry or determined, his dark brown eyes turned nearly black, intimidating his opponents into submission, but she was equally determined that no man, not even Jess Logan, was going to intimidate her. "You can talk until you're blue in the face," she said the moment the door closed behind Morning Hawk, "but I'm not taking this job."

Breaking his gaze from hers, Jess drew a terse breath. "Look, I don't like this any better than you do, but when my great-grandmother sets her mind to something, she can make a person's life miserable until she gets her way. I'll pay you ten thousand dollars to find three reasonably pleasant women for me to take out on a couple of dates each. That way, I'll have lived up to my end of the bargain and Morning Hawk will have to live up to hers."

"I'm not interested in taking your money."

Jess scowled. "Next to my great-grandmother, you are the most stubborn, bullheaded woman I've ever known. No, I take that back. You're even more stubborn and bullheaded than she is.''

"I'll take that as a compliment. Now if you'll excuse me, I've business elsewhere." Gwen started to the door, inwardly relieved that she'd delivered her exit line and could be on her way.

But before she had gone two paces, Jess's hand closed around her arm, bringing her to a halt. His calluses were rough against her skin but instead of feeling abrasive, they caused an intense sensual stirring deep within. She rebelled against this sensation. *I am not my mother,* she seethed at herself. Aloud she snapped, "Let go of me," and attempted to twist free.

Jess released her and held up his hand in a sign of peace. "Okay, okay. I didn't want to turn this into another of our skirmishes. All I want is to pacify Morning Hawk." A dry smile curled one corner of his mouth. "And save you some trouble. She's got her mind set on you doing this for her and she'll pester you until you do. Believe me, I know."

Gwen held her arms stiffly at her sides, fighting the urge to rub off the lingering effect of his touch while she considered his words. She guessed he was right. It was common knowledge that when Morning Hawk set her mind to something, it remained set. Besides, she did owe the woman for talking her out of doing something that could have proved to be very foolish. This would clear up that debt, then she would never have to have anything to do with any of the Logans or their kin again. "Okay," she agreed grudgingly. "But I won't take your money. I'll bill your grandmother for my time like I would any other client. And," she added firmly, "I'll do my best to find suitable candidates. I hope you'll treat them with respect."

"I always treat women with respect."

Gwen gave him a dry look, then strode out of the room. A curl of guilt wove through her. The skeptical glance she'd tossed at him had been unfair. The truth was she had no reason to doubt his statement. In fact, she had every reason to accept it as fact. She'd never known him to treat anyone with disrespect unless they deserved it.

Morning Hawk was waiting on the porch. "Well, will you accept my quest?"

"I'll find three candidates."

Morning Hawk grinned widely. "I'm sure you'll seek out the perfect wife for my great-grandson." Her manner became businesslike. "Do you want to move in tonight or wait until tomorrow?"

Gwen stared. "Move in?" she finally managed to choke out.

"Well, of course. You have to get to know Jess before you can find a match for him."

"I don't think getting to know him will prove useful. You can both just give me a list of criteria and I'll go from there."

"Don't be ridiculous. To do the job right will require much more knowledge than what we can put on paper."

"Really, Great-Grandma." Jess stepped out onto the porch. Obviously he'd been listening from the hall and decided that his intervention was necessary. "There's no reason for Gwen to move in."

"This is your life. She must understand it and you to find the right woman for you."

It was clear to Gwen from the expression on Jess's face that he didn't like the idea of her living under his roof any more than she did. "I'm sure Jess has a very good idea of the wife he wants. He can simply describe her to me and I'll go from there.''

"Fantasies never work out well. He needs a real woman who will fit into his life." Morning Hawk's tone became sterner. "And not one who's simply after his money.''

"I'm not stupid enough to be taken in by a gold digger," Jess growled.

Morning Hawk tossed him an indulgent look. "Any man can be taken in by a pretty face and good figure. And that's what the service Gwen provides will protect against. She goes beyond face value. Anyone she finds for you will be trustworthy as well as fit your requirements.''

Jess breathed a resigned sigh. "She can move in today. The sooner we get started, the better.''

"I really d—" Gwen started to protest.

"A person could get the idea that you're afraid of sharing the same roof with me," Jess cut her off, challenge again in his eyes.

Gwen's shoulders stiffened. "I'm most certainly not intimidated by the likes of you, Jess Logan." Heading to her car, she added over her shoulder, "I'll go get my things and be back in a couple of hours.''

Driving away, she glanced in her rearview mirror to see Jess stalk back into the house. She rolled her eyes toward the heavens. "I can't believe I'm doing this.'' Abruptly, a crooked grin tilted one corner of her mouth. She wasn't alone. Both she and Jess Logan had been manipulated by Morning Hawk. And the thought of him being maneuvered into a corner by the elderly woman made the situation laughable. *Almost* laughable, she corrected, reminding herself that she was in the same corner.

Chapter Two

An uneasy feeling ran through Gwen as she parked in front of the Logan ranch house later that day. Her father had exited her life even before she was born. When she was seventeen, her mother had died. Since then, she'd lived alone and grown used to her solitary existence.

"I had Lilly make up a room for you." Jess greeted her, coming out of the house and heading to her car.

"Lilly?" Gwen had been under the impression Jess and Morning Hawk were the only people occupying the house.

"Our housekeeper. Lilly Chambers," Jess elaborated. "She was in town doing some grocery shopping when you were here earlier."

Gwen chided herself mentally. Of course the Logans would have a housekeeper. "Thanks," she replied curtly, using terseness to hide her growing nervousness.

"Look, I'm not any happier about this than you are," he returned with equal animosity, "but we've made a bargain and we might as well be civil about it.''

"I'm used to living alone." She tried to school the tenseness out of her voice but an edge remained. Not wanting him to guess how uneasy he made her, especially after that unnerving reaction she'd had to his touch, she added, "I guess I'm a little short on people skills.''

"You always have been."

She bit back a retort. She had good reason for being the way she was, but that was her own private hell and no one else's and she had no intention of revealing it just to justify her behavior.

Jess's eyebrow raised in a questioning arch when she made no response. Then obviously accepting her silence as an end to the conversation, he picked up her satchel and computer bag.

Gwen grabbed at it. "I can carry my own things."

"My mother taught me to be polite to guests."

"Well, I'm no guest. I'm an employee."

"You're a female. I'd never hear the end of it from the women in my family if I didn't carry your bag."

Realizing she was fighting a losing battle, she shrugged and reached into the car for the old wooden baseball bat lying on the floor.

Surprise showed on Jess's face. "Don't you think that's overreacting a bit. I'm just trying to be a good host.''

A flush reddened her cheeks. "I wasn't going to use it on you."

A grin tilted one corner of his mouth. "Never thought I'd hear myself saying this, but you look kind of cute when you're flustered."

Abruptly, her eyes turned cold with warning. "I'd

better correct my last statement. I'm not planning to use this bat on you right now. But I do plan to keep it around in case any varmints wander too close.''

"Cute like a rattlesnake," Jess muttered, clearly rethinking his first reaction. He met her icy glare with impatience. "Well, you don't have to worry about me."

"Good." A curl of self-directed anger wove through her. He'd just told her what she wanted to hear. She should have been relieved, but deep inside she'd felt a sting. *I'm just overly tense,* she reasoned, pushing the car door closed.

Leading the way into the house, Jess silently cursed his great-grandmother for inviting this woman under their roof. She'd always been as prickly as a cactus and the fact that she thought she needed a bat to protect herself from him grated on his nerves. He sure as heck had never given her any indication he found her the least bit attractive. Not that she wasn't physically good-looking…nice figure, curves in all the right places, green eyes and chestnut hair cut short so that it framed her face in a gentle style. But her core was cold as ice and hard as stone.

After showing her to her room, he went in search of Morning Hawk and found her in the kitchen with Lilly.

"I've got a stew on the stove and will be putting the corn bread in shortly," Lilly said. She was in her mid-fifties, comfortable in her manner and she had a kindly disposition.

"Thanks." Jess gave her the barest of glances. Lilly had worked for the Logans since she was a teenager. He considered her a trustworthy part of their household and thus felt perfectly comfortable discussing Gwen in front of her. Locking his gaze on Morning Hawk, he said tersely, "I don't think inviting Gwen to stay under our roof was such a good idea."

"She's not as difficult to get along with as some people think," Lilly spoke.

Surprised by the housekeeper's defense of his unwanted guest, Jess's gaze swung to her.

"She kept my niece from getting involved with a real loser. My sister didn't like the guy so she hired Gwen to check him out. Turned out he not only had a criminal record, he had two wives and a total of six kids."

"I'm not saying that what she does isn't useful." Jess's gaze traveled between the two women. His jaw tensed. "She keeps a baseball bat with her."

Morning Hawk regarded him indulgently. "A woman who lives alone should have something to protect herself with."

Lilly nodded. "A lot of young women have taken to carrying guns. Not that I think that's such a good idea. But on the other hand, the world has become a much more dangerous place, or so it seems. My daughter has taken up karate and she's already up to a brown belt."

"Maybe I should take some self-defense courses before I go out on my next date. And maybe carry a metal detector with me," Jess muttered, shaking his head as he left the kitchen and went to his study.

Seated at his desk, he doodled on the edges of a sheet of paper where he'd listed a number of women's names. He had nothing against marriage. He just hadn't met the woman he wanted to spend the rest of his life with. Even more, he didn't like being pushed! "I'll find a wife myself and in my own sweet time," he growled, then focused his full attention on the paper in front of him.

After Gwen had left, he'd given this current situation a great deal of thought. He didn't like blind dates. If he was going to go out with someone, it was going to be someone he had, at least, a passing acquaintance with. His plan was to hand Gwen the names of three women and tell her to set him up with them. That would make his part a bit more palatable and hers easy, allowing them to get finished with this charade quickly. Stopping his doodling, he made his final list.

Gwen stood at the window in her bedroom, knowing she had to leave the sanctity of the room and face Jess but not wanting to. She'd never understood why he had such a strong effect on her. He just did.

Her mind went back to her first day in school after she and her mother had moved to this panhandle area of Texas. She'd been in fourth grade. When it came time for lunch, a couple of the popular girls had attached themselves to her, more to find out all about her than to claim her as a friend. The three of them were just finishing eating when Jess wandered over to introduce himself. The other two girls had twittered, clearly excited and pleased by his presence. He was two years older and the fact that he was welcoming Gwen was clearly an event as far as her friends were concerned. But he made her feel weirdly uncomfortable in ways she'd never felt before and that had scared her. To hide her discomfort, she'd given him a cold look that told him she didn't want him anywhere near her. The two girls she'd been eating with were both stunned and quickly made excuses to get away from her. From then on she'd been excluded from the popular crowd. But she didn't care. They would have expected her to invite them to her house and she never invited anyone there.

In addition to the house always smelling like liquor and stale cigarettes, her mother was a lousy housekeeper. Bottles and full ashtrays littered all the rooms except for Gwen's and she never knew when her mother might come home early from work with a new "friend."

Even Henry, the one lasting friend she'd made while in school here and who she'd learned to love like a brother, had only been inside a few times. His home life had been as bad as hers in its own way, so she hadn't been quite so embarrassed about him coming in. Still, the uncertainty of finding her mother drunk or with a "friend" caused her to check the house before she let even him enter.

A knock on Gwen's door startled her, jerking her mind back to the present. Answering the summons, she found her nemesis standing there.

"I suppose I should be flattered that you didn't answer with your weapon in your hand," he muttered.

Again a tint of red colored her cheeks. She'd tried to make herself leave the bat behind, but it had been her security blanket from an early age and she couldn't sleep without it under her bed. "You said I was safe from you and from what I've heard, Logans keep their word."

Jess nodded to emphasize this point, then extended a piece of paper toward her. "I've decided to make your job a lot easier by providing you with the names of three women you can set me up with."

"I suppose they're ones who will be totally disagreeable to your great-grandmother, so she won't get any more ideas about matchmaking."

"No. Morning Hawk would never believe you would find anyone totally unsuitable. They're women I might consider marrying if I was of a mind to get married. After you've stuck around here for a couple of days, you can say you know enough about me and we can get on to the dating phase of this.''

Before Gwen could respond, he strode away. Closing her door, she stared at the names he'd given her.

For a moment she was surprised that Jeanette Harrison wasn't at the top of the list. Then recalling the exchange between Jess and Morning Hawk, she realized he was excluding her because he knew Morning Hawk considered her unsuitable and he wanted this little game to flow easily and quickly to its finish.

And it should, she thought as she reviewed the list. She knew all three women to some extent. Each had been born and raised in this rural community of which the Logan land was a part. And they'd all attended the same grade school and high school as she and Jess. After high school, they'd continued their educations and eventually settled in and around Lubbock.

The first was Susan O'Rilley...a tall, slender redhead who was not only beautiful, but very clever and highly intelligent. She had a law degree from Harvard. Currently she was an assistant district attorney in Lubbock, and there were a lot of people who believed she would eventually be top dog.

Next was Mary Beth Lloyd, pretty, medium build, a brunette, also college educated. She taught grade school and had a motherly aura.

The last was Brenda Jackson, a blonde with curves in all the right places. She was a nurse, and a great many of her male patients said she'd given them a new lease on life just by walking into their rooms and smiling at them. Gwen had even heard her referred to as ''that healing angel'' and ''the angel in white.''

''This list should please Morning Hawk.'' Still, the

whole business grated on her nerves. Abruptly, she squared her shoulders. "I can't stay in here forever." Opening the door, she stepped out into the hall.

"So where to now?" she murmured under her breath. Old habits died hard. Without even making a conscious decision, she headed away from the main part of the house, casing out the hall on which her room was located. She'd always felt safer when she knew her surroundings. There were three other bedrooms there. The first two she peered into had a vacant feel to them. Pictures and mementos on the bureaus led her to believe they had belonged to Slade and Boyd Logan, Jess's older brothers. And she guessed they were kept in readiness for visits from either of them and their wives. The third door was the one next to hers on her side of the hall.

Opening it, she looked around cautiously. It had a lived-in look. There was a shirt hung over a chair and the mild scent of aftershave lingered in the air. Without any doubt, she knew this was Jess's room. As if she'd uncovered a rattlesnake's lair, she took a step back and pulled the door closed.

"Looking for me?"

The sound of Jess's voice startled her. Turning to face him, she ordered herself to appear calm. "No. I was merely checking out my environment. You know, escape routes in case of fire and such."

"There's a window in your bedroom and we're on the ground level."

"So I might be somewhere else."

A sarcastic smirk tilted one corner of his mouth. "My room?"

"I didn't know it was your room before I opened the door. And I can tell you this will be the one and only time I do that.'' With a look that said this was a promise, she strode past him and down the hall.

In spite of the air of relaxed comfort the decor of the house portrayed, Gwen felt out of place. Deciding to make herself useful, she headed to the kitchen to offer assistance.

Lilly greeted her with a smile. ''Morning Hawk told me why you're here and swore me to secrecy. I'm supposed to tell everyone that you're helping her with some sort of genealogy search.''

''Sounds like a good cover.''

Lilly shook her head. ''I don't know what's gotten into her. It's not like her to mettle in her great-grandsons' lives like this. And it's not like the family was worried Jess would never get married. He's got nothing against marriage.'' Her expression took on a hint of apology. ''I'm not saying your services aren't valuable. In fact, I was telling Jess earlier today how you helped out my niece. But hiring a matchmaker. I can't believe Jess is going along with it.''

''He didn't have a choice.''

Lilly nodded solemnly with understanding. ''When his great-grandma gets a bee in her bonnet, generally humoring her is the best way to handle it. Sometimes, it's the only way. And she did tell me that he only has to date the women you pick. She's not actually insisting that he marry any of them.''

''That's right,'' Gwen confirmed.

''Well, I guess it's all right then. I just hate to see her putting Jess through all of this on a whim.'' A puzzled expression came over her features. ''What's really peculiar is that I've never known her to do anything on a whim.'' Again she shook her head. ''Never thought I'd see the day when she got senile. But maybe this is the first sign. Some people think she's always been a bit wacky, but it's been my experience that there's generally a good reason behind everything she does.''

"She did say she wanted to see Jess married before she met her maker. Maybe she's suddenly gotten worried about her mortality and this crazy idea sprung out of that." Gwen offered an explanation for Morning Hawk's behavior. "People can get a bit eccentric when they finally face the fact that they're not going to live forever."

Lilly nodded vigorously. "That's true."

Not wanting to discuss Jess or his great-grandmother any further, Gwen changed the subject to her original purpose. "Can I give you a hand with dinner?"

Lilly shook her head. "Oh, no. You're a guest."

"I'm an employee just like you," Gwen corrected. "And right this minute I need to feel useful."

For a moment Lilly made no response, then said, "If you really don't mind, I would like to get home a little early. Bobbie, my grandson, has a baseball game tonight and I told him I'd try to get there to see him pitch."

Gwen had hoped that Lilly was live-in help. The more people around, the better. Then chiding herself for this bit of totally unnecessary cowardliness, she forced a smile. "No problem. What do you want me to do?"

"I've cooked a stew." As she spoke, Lilly lifted the lid of a heavy iron pot on the stove and gave the contents a stir. With a shrug of her shoulder toward the long heavy wooden table in the center of the large kitchen, she added, "And the table is set. All that's left is to take the corn bread out of the oven. When the timer goes off it should be ready.''

''I know how to tell if it's done,'' Gwen assured her. ''You run along.''

Lilly hesitated. ''Are you sure?''

''Yes, now go.''

Lilly was heading for the door when Jess entered.

''I told her to leave and let me finish putting the meal on the table,'' Gwen said hurriedly, uncertain how strict Jess was about his help leaving early and not wanting to be the cause of any anger toward Lilly.

''I was just coming in to offer the same service,'' Jess returned in an easy drawl, giving the housekeeper a friendly smile. ''You run along and go see Bobbie pitch.''

''Thanks.'' Lilly grinned back, then hurried on her way.

Surprised that Jess had been willing to take over kitchen duties, but wanting him to leave, Gwen said, ''I can take care of things in here. You go back to whatever you usually do before dinner.''

''Fixing dinner isn't your job.''

The need to feel useful was too strong for Gwen to retreat. ''I told Lilly I'd do it. Now, just go away and let me take care of things here.'' Suddenly realizing she was trying to order Jess Logan around in his own home, she hid her embarrassment behind a shield of angry impatience.

For a long moment, Jess studied her, then a small crooked grin tilted one corner of his mouth. ''I'd offer to arm wrestle you for it, but I figure I'd better keep my distance. As I recall, the last time I saw someone get you riled it was Joe Jackson and you punched him so hard in the stomach, you got yourself suspended from school for three days.''

Gwen recalled the incident vividly. It had happened during her sophomore year in high school. The minute she'd thrown the punch, she'd known it was the wrong thing to do and truly felt horrible about it. But Joe had hit a tender nerve...a very tender nerve. He'd whispered in her ear that he'd heard her mother was "easy" and could be had for a couple of drinks. Then he'd wanted to know what Gwen's price was. Her shoulders straightened with defiance. "Joe Jackson had a vulgar mouth.''

"True. But most girls would have just slapped him or given him a nasty look and walked away.''

"That would only have egged him on.'' Fighting down a surge of old guilt at her act of violence, she added in her defense, "He needed to be taught a lesson.''

"You're right. He did.''

Gwen had expected Jess to continue mocking her behavior. That he agreed with her, startled her. Adding to her surprise, he grinned.

"I can still see the look on Joe's face,'' he said. "He always bullied you girls because he never expected you to respond the way you did.''

A haunted shadow flitted in Gwen's eyes. "His type only prey on those weaker than themselves.''

Jess's smile vanished and his gaze narrowed on her. "You sound like you've had more than your share of experience with his type.''

Angry that she'd nearly revealed things she was determined to keep private, she said with cool calm, "All women have had experience with his type. Some are just slower learners than others. That's what keeps me in business." Not wanting this conversation to continue, she turned her attention to the timer on the stove. "Looks like it's getting to be time to pour the drinks." Realizing he wasn't leaving, she added, "Since you came to work and you know more about where things are in this kitchen, you can do that. I'll take water."

Gwen could feel Jess staring at her. Her breath locked in lungs as she waited for him to make some snide remark about her ordering him around in his own kitchen. Then the sensation was gone and she heard him moving around the room, finding glasses and filling them.

Neither spoke except for the necessary communications involved in getting the dinner on the table and summoning Morning Hawk. As all three seated themselves and they began to dish food onto their plates, the stilted atmosphere remained.

Morning Hawk's gaze traveled between them. "Obviously the two of you haven't decided to be social to one another yet, but I am relieved you can be left alone in a room full of weapons and not get into a fight."

Jess's eyes leveled on Gwen. "I tried to make small talk but she was like a wet cat. She snapped at everything I said."

Gwen met his gaze. "You were being nosy."

"All right, so maybe I was."

Gwen's eyes rounded. "You admit it?"

"I realized a long time ago that your coldness wasn't limited just to me. You seem to hold a grudge against men in general. I was just curious as to why."

Gwen's jaw hardened. "Men are users."

"Not all men."

"I suppose. But it's hard to know which are and which aren't. To avoid any trouble, I prefer to assume the worst and steer clear.'' Immediately, she regretted not keeping her mouth shut. Jess was regarding her so narrowly his gaze felt like a knife trying to pierce the thick skin she'd grown around herself. Refusing to allow this conversation to remain on her, she added in a calm tone, ''But then some women are users as well. I'm assuming that's why I'm here. To make sure you don't get hooked by one of them.''

Jess's attention turned to his great-grandmother. ''I've always considered myself real good at telling a shark from a trout.''

Morning Hawk smiled. ''Sometimes a man's vision can be so blurred by the beauty and excitement of the moment, he's sunk the hook before he realizes he's snagged a fish not worth reeling in.''

''When I'm doing some serious fishing, I always cast my line carefully,'' Jess assured her.

Morning Hawk's expression became that of a wise sage. ''No one can be certain about what lies beneath still waters.''

Jess shook his head in a gesture of defeat and turned his attention to his food.

Gwen breathed a mental sigh of relief as silence again settled over the table.

A couple of hours later, Gwen plopped into the chair in her bedroom.

Following the meal, Jess had insisted on helping her clean up the kitchen.

''I'm sure the two of you don't need my help,'' Morning Hawk had said, and headed for the door. Then as if she'd had second thoughts, she'd seated herself in a rocking chair by the potbellied stove and taken out some handwork she kept in a basket there.

Gwen had the impression the elderly woman had decided that a peacemaker or, perhaps, a referee might be needed.

But as it turned out, the cleaning up had gone smoothly. She and Jess had kept their conversation focused on getting the job done and afterward he'd retired to his study and Gwen had taken refuge in her room.

Drawing in a deep breath to calm her taut nerves, she realized she hadn't locked her door. Something was definitely wrong with her survival instinct. From an early age, she'd always locked her door. Rising, she flipped the latch, then reseating herself, she frowned.

When she and Jess were cleaning the kitchen, his arm had brushed hers a couple of times and each time she'd felt as if she'd been shocked by a bolt of electricity. And then there was that moment at the table when he'd admitted he'd been prying. The tiniest hint of an embarrassed smile had played at one corner of his mouth and she'd found herself thinking that he looked boyishly handsome. There had even been a momentary weakening in her knees. This was not good. Her mother had always been feeling weak in the knees about one man or another, and that was something Gwen had vowed never to do.

"Clearly, I'm just overly tense," she reasoned. "I'm not used to living under the same roof with strangers or with anyone else for that matter. I just need a good night's sleep."

But even as she muttered these words, she was sure attempting to sleep would prove futile. However, a short while later, after a final check to make sure her bat was within reach, she crawled under the covers and closed her eyes. Almost immediately she fell into a comfortable slumber.

Chapter Three

Gwen opened her eyes to discover sunlight streaming in her window. She couldn't believe it. In a strange house with a man who unnerved her merely by his presence, she'd had one of the best night's sleeps she'd had in her life. "I'm definitely losing my edge," she grumbled, throwing off the covers.

Entering the kitchen a short while later, she found Morning Hawk sitting at the table drinking coffee. Jess was nowhere in sight.

"He's out riding fences," Morning Hawk said, as if sensing the trail of Gwen's thoughts. Nodding toward the refrigerator, she added, "Lilly won't be here until a bit later. We get our own breakfast around here. There's eggs, ham and bacon. Make whatever you want."

Gwen started to say she wasn't hungry, then her stomach growled and she realized she was. "Thanks." Opening the refrigerator, she took out a couple of eggs and the ham.

Watching her slice off a piece of the meat, Morning Hawk said, "I assume Jess gave you a list of names you're supposed to pretend you chose for him."

Gwen looked over her shoulder. "Does anything ever get by you?"

"Not where my great-grandsons are concerned. At least, not Jess."

Gwen turned, leaned against the counter, crossed her arms and regarded Morning Hawk wryly. "If you knew that was what he would do, why this charade?"

"Because without some prodding, he wasn't going to do any serious wife hunting and I want to see him settled before I go to the great hunting grounds in the sky."

"But this isn't serious wife hunting. You're both just playing a game with each other."

"Did he put Jeanette Harrison's name on the list?"

"No."

"Then it's serious wife hunting."

"He left the name off because he knew you would protest."

"He left the name off because, deep down inside, he knows she's not good wife material."

Gwen straightened. "Look, I didn't like taking money for this charade before, but now that I know you're not being fooled, I refuse to play this game."

"But it's not a game. Whether you're willing to believe it or not, these are women Jess thinks he could marry. And I want you to investigate them just as you would if you were playing matchmaker for one of your regular clients."

"I don't play matchmaker for my clients. I merely tell them if what they see is what they're getting or if there's a hidden side to the person they're dating that they should be aware of.''

Morning Hawk rose, approached Gwen and took her hands in hers. ''Please, do this for me and promise me that you won't tell Jess I've guessed his game.''

''I don't feel right taking money for this.''

''Don't be silly. You'll be doing your usual investigation.'' Morning Hawk's expression became sage. ''Besides, if this prodding of mine does make him decide to get married, you wouldn't want to let him fall into the clutches of the wrong woman just because you refused to help me weed out the bad ones.''

Gwen wanted to say that she was sure Jess could take care of himself, but Morning Hawk had planted just enough of the seed of guilt to force her to admit that if he did pick unwisely it could be partially her fault. ''Even if we warn him, I doubt he'll listen to us,'' she said, wishing she'd never gotten involved in this in the first place.

''At least we'll know we tried,'' Morning Hawk countered. ''Now I want your promise that you'll keep this conversation between the two of us.''

''I owe you a large debt, but you're asking a lot. I don't like to deal in lies.''

''These are just little white ones and for a good cause.''

''I'm not so sure Jess would see it that way.''

''Please. I've communicated with the spirits and they're leading me now just as they led you to me years ago.''

Memories of that dark night so long ago when fear had caused Gwen to run from her home came vividly back to Gwen's mind.

"Promise me you'll see this through," Morning Hawk coaxed.

"It's against my better judgment, but all right," Gwen relented, adding, "I wouldn't do this if I didn't owe you so much."

"You'll see, you're doing the right thing." Morning Hawk gave Gwen's hands a motherly squeeze. "Now eat some breakfast. You've got work to do."

Gwen leaned back in her chair and stretched. She'd moved a table and chair into her bedroom and set up her computer there, then spent all morning checking the easily available records pertaining to the women Jess had chosen.

At first, she'd locked her door. But both Lilly and Morning Hawk had dropped by to see her for various reasons and, not only had it been inconvenient to have to get up and unlock the door each time one of them knocked, but the look of surprise they'd given her when they'd discovered she had locked the door had made her feel foolish. And so, in the end, she'd not only left the door unlocked but open as well.

Bootfalls in the hall warned her of someone approaching. Even before she turned her head to see who had come to a halt in the doorway of her room, she knew it was Jess. The hairs on the back of her neck had always prickled slightly when he was around and right now they felt like the spines on a cactus. Suddenly she found herself wishing the door was not only locked but bolted as well. Silently she cursed herself for allowing him to have such a strong effect on her.

"You sure you aren't cramped in here?" he asked.

Gwen turned and grinned dryly. "You've never been

in one of the rooms at Mrs. O'Grady's boardinghouse, have you?''

"Can't say as I have."

No, of course he wouldn't have ever been there, she mocked herself, her grin vanishing. Mrs. O'Grady ran a clean, respectable place but it was way across the tracks from anywhere the Logans would go. Except maybe Jess's brothers. They'd probably been in the neighborhood chasing down criminals. She rose, her manner crisply businesslike. "This room suits me just fine."

Jess studied her. "Sounds like you've lived in some pretty tough neighborhoods. Now I understand the bat."

She met his gaze. "You don't understand anything." The moment the words were out, she regretted them.

Jess's gaze narrowed. "What don't I understand?"

"Look, I'm hungry. I'm going to see if Lilly has lunch ready." Her tone let him know she considered their conversation over.

Jess shook his head. "I've never met a woman as closemouthed as you."

"Most men would be grateful for that. Isn't 'women talking too much' one of your major complaints?" He was still blocking the doorway. Normally she would have pushed past, but recalling the effect of contact with him, she chose not to get too close. "Would you mind moving out of my way?"

Jess took a couple of paces back into the hall.

Passing him, she headed toward the kitchen, only to hear his footfalls behind her. She glanced impatiently over her shoulder, then stopped and turned back. "Do you have some reason for dogging my tracks?"

"I came to tell you that Lilly has lunch ready," he replied in an easy drawl.

As usual, in Jess Logan's presence, she'd overreacted. She handled being around other men just fine...always remaining in cool control. But he seemed to bring out the worst in her, causing her to suddenly be terse and impolite. *It's not him; it's me,* she admitted grudgingly. Something about him threatened her control. He was so darn...virile. This thought shook her and she shoved it from her mind. "Thanks," she said in a level tone. Wanting to put distance between them, she again started down the hall.

Jess fell into step beside her. "Didn't you get bored sitting in that room all morning? You could have said you wanted to do some visual surveillance and run into town."

"I was doing my preliminary workups."

He frowned. "What for? This is just a game to pacify Morning Hawk."

"She'll expect to see some paperwork."

"She may, but I don't. I figure if I'm interested enough in a person, I'll find out what I need to know myself, in my own way."

"That's exactly what a lot of the women I end up working for said the first, second and third times around before they finally realized how devious some people can be and came to me."

"I'm not the victim type."

Gwen had to admit that was her feeling, too. Still, a cautionary cord in her caused her to say, "Anyone can be a victim when it comes to love."

"I suppose. But I'm willing to take my chances."

She told herself to drop the subject, but heard herself

countering with, "Don't forget the old adage, The bigger they are, the harder they fall."

"So, I'll just have to make sure that when I fall, the woman I choose will be the kind who won't let me get hurt."

Gwen found herself hoping that same thing. What startled her was the strength of that hope. It came very close to feeling actually protective of him.

"You got hurt? A fence barb get you?" Morning Hawk questioned sharply, catching the last three words as Gwen and Jess entered the kitchen. "Let me see."

"We were talking about women." Jess's gaze leveled on his great-grandmother. "I don't intend to get hurt by one. And especially not because I let someone push me into something I'm not ready for."

"I'm just giving you a little nudge. I'm not shoving you off a cliff."

Lilly eyed the group, her hands on her hips. "If you ask me, I think Jess should be left alone and allowed to get married when he's ready and not before."

Jess gave Lilly an approving look. "Thanks."

Lilly's gaze focused on Morning Hawk. "Meddling in other people's business, especially their love life, can bring results you least expect," she warned. Then clamping her lips shut to indicate she'd said all she felt she needed to say on this subject, she returned to putting food on the table.

Morning Hawk regarded the housekeeper indulgently, then turned to Gwen. "You should go out with Jess this afternoon. You need to know as much about him as possible to find the right match."

"I really don't think tagging along after him is necessary," Gwen protested, silently cursing the elderly woman for what she considered pushing this charade much further than was necessary. "Besides, I don't know how to ride."

Morning Hawk regarded her patronizingly. "Then it's time you did."

"I really…"

"You might as well give up now," Jess interrupted. "She's not going to stop until she has her way."

"But I'm sure you're much too busy to teach me how to handle a horse."

"I feel certain you of all people will pick it up very quickly," Jess returned. "All you need to do to make a horse behave is let him know that you're not scared of him and consider yourself in command. You're too tough to be afraid or to give an inch in your authority."

He made her sound hard as nails. And the truth was that she prided herself on being just that. But for some reason, hearing him say it made her feel subhuman. "Some people don't have it as easy as others. They have to learn to be tough to survive." Immediately she clamped her mouth shut. Why was she always blurting out things in front of him that she'd never said aloud to anyone else before? *Beetles,* she cursed mentally.

"I didn't mean to sound critical," Jess apologized. Then he added, "Well, maybe I did a little. I'm used to women showing at least a semblance of a soft side."

Back in control, Gwen managed a shrug of indifference. "Well, just consider me one of the guys."

"That's an excellent idea." Morning Hawk broke in, smiling broadly at Gwen and then turning her grin on Jess. "Men always tell each other things they wouldn't tell a female and Gwen needs to know as much about you as possible to find the perfect match."

Both Gwen and Jess frowned at her delight, then turned their attention to their food.

Chapter Four

With an outward show of confidence to mask her inward trepidation, Gwen entered the fenced grazing area adjacent to the stables with Jess. Jess whistled. A large black stallion looked their way. Gwen had the distinct feeling the animal had known they were there all along, but was waiting to hear them announce themselves. Then with an easy grace, the horse turned in their direction and approached.

Gwen took an involuntary step backward as the animal reached Jess and bent his head toward the cowboy.

"Afternoon, Raven. Looks like we're going to have company on this ride." In an aside to Gwen, Jess added, "He won't bite. You can step forward again."

She hated the fact that she'd shown even a moment's cowardliness in front of him. With a long step closer, she placed herself right next to the beast. "Good boy," she said firmly, and patted his neck the way she's seen people do in the movies.

"I can't believe you live in Texas and haven't learned to ride," Jess commented, as he slipped the lead halter on Raven.

Raven moved slightly and, with every ounce of control she could muster, Gwen managed to stop herself from jumping away. Instead, she sidestepped as gracefully as her shaky legs would allow. "I've never had any need to."

Jess smiled. "I told you there's no reason to be skittish around Raven. He's a lot gentler than he looks."

Gwen continued to eye the horse cautiously. "I prefer to stay away from anything too big for me to throw."

Jess's smile broadened. "So that's why you've always kept me at arm's length."

A confident smiled curled one corner of her mouth. "Oh, I can throw you. I have a black belt in karate."

Jess continued to grin. "Maybe someday we'll just have to see about that."

Gwen had never felt so tightly strung and the temptation to release some of her tension by proving to him right then and there that she wasn't being flippant was strong. But even as her body prepared to toss him, something deeper stopped her. It was a very peculiar reaction to the thought of physical contact…something between excitement and terror. Again she recalled sharply the effect his hand had had on her arm and the currents of electricity his simple brushing against her in the kitchen had sent through her body. Drawing a deep breath, she shut down her body's fight mode. "I don't think so. I wouldn't want you to get hurt."

Jess's smile vanished, and he regarded her narrowly. "Don't you ever joke or have any fun?"

"Not when I'm on a job."

Jess turned to Raven. "I'd watch my step with her," he warned the animal.

Raven snorted and nodded his head as if he'd understood.

Jess turned back to Gwen. "I'll cut Lady Grace out for you. She has an easy lope." Swinging up onto Raven's bare back, he nudged the horse and they headed to the far side of the fenced area.

"Raven and his master are well paired," she muttered, recalling the animal's almost human reaction to Jess's warning. Well, he and his master could mock her all they wanted. What any male thought about her—what any person thought, she corrected—didn't matter to her.

A strong nudge on the middle of her back sent her forward. "What do you—" she growled, turning around to confront her assailant. The words died when she found herself face-to-face with a chestnut horse. And there was, she was sure, a mischievous glint in his eyes.

In spite of the animal's size, she found herself thinking that he was like a little boy, playing a game. "Don't think you can get away with pushing me around," she warned him sternly.

He cocked his head to one side as if sizing her up.

Remembering what Jess had told her about handling horses, she placed her hands on her hips and said curtly. "Behave yourself."

The chestnut straightened and took a step forward.

"Oh, great. A horse who bucks authority," she muttered. Unable to stop herself, she took a step back only to find herself up against the fence.

The horse nudged her shoulder gently, then stepped back.

Suddenly realizing he was asking to be her friend, Gwen experienced an overwhelming sense of delight. "Okay, tough guy," she said, moving forward and patting his neck. "Or should I say tough gal?"

"Tough guy was correct," Jess said riding up with a gray mare on a lead rope.

Gwen continued to grin at the chestnut. "So, what's his name."

"Cantankerous."

"Cantankerous?"

Jess dismounted. "He earned it." Nodding toward the stables, he added, "Come on. We'll get these horses saddled and you can have your first lesson."

"See you later, buddy," Gwen said, giving the chestnut a final pat on the neck, before falling into step beside Jess.

The gray she noticed seemed almost lethargic and definitely disinterested in her. *An elitist,* she decided. She'd never been fond of elitists. Out of the corner of her eye, she noticed that Cantankerous was following and a hint of a smile played at the corner of her mouth.

"I'd rather ride the chestnut," she heard herself saying without even realizing she'd been going to speak aloud. Inwardly, a nervous twinge spiked through her. What did she think she was doing? She was a novice rider. She didn't need a horse that was unpredictable.

Jess frowned. "I'm not so sure that's a good idea."

"I thought cowboys were supposed to feel a bond with their mounts. Well, I sort of feel that with Cantankerous." She couldn't believe she was arguing with him over which horse she should ride. She was no judge of horseflesh. Still, she thought she saw a plea in the chestnut's eyes asking her to choose him.

"I suppose there could be a personality match between the two of you," Jess conceded.

Gwen gave him a dry look. Then in a moment of honesty, she heard herself saying, "You could be right."

Jess regarded her thoughtfully. "So you are capable of not taking yourself too seriously all of the time."

"I have my moments," she replied.

"Great." He grinned. "There's hope for you yet."

His approval caused a warm glow to spread through her. So, maybe she did take everything a bit too seriously. Immediately her jaw tensed. She'd had to learn to be hard in order to survive. "I think I'm doing just fine exactly as I am."

Jess frowned with impatience. "I was only suggesting that you could lighten up a little bit."

Her shoulders stiffened with dignity. "And I choose to stay the way I am."

"Stubborn," Jess muttered, releasing Lady Grace.

Gwen breathed a sigh of relief as he turned his full attention to saddling the horses. In spite of her bravado, he made her want to relax her defenses and show the softer, more vulnerable side she kept hidden from view. Fear suddenly washed through her. *No,* her inner voice ordered. Every instinct screamed that lowering her defenses could be dangerous and the protective shield she kept around herself once again solidified.

"Time to mount," Jess announced, cutting into her thoughts. "Always from the left," he added.

"That part I know." Rounding the horse, she grasped the horn of the saddle and tried to get her foot up into the stirrup. It was a stretch she couldn't quite make. "I didn't realize how tall he was," she said looking around for a bucket to give her some height.

"Here, I'll give you a hand up." Jess cupped his hands in the shape of an open stirrup. "Hold on to the horn and get ready to swing up into the saddle when I give you a lift."

Gwen nodded, firmed her hold on the horn, then slipped her foot into his hands. The contact unexpectedly caused her legs to weaken. She couldn't believe it. He was wearing heavy gloves and she was wearing boots, yet heat was rushing through her as if they were touching skin against skin.

"Here goes." Jess gave her a firm lift upward.

Still distracted by the effect he had on her, she floundered, missed getting her seating in the saddle and began sliding downward.

Jess caught her under the arms. As she released the horn, her body swung against his and she grasped his shoulders for support.

"Guess you weren't quite ready," he said with apology.

His hands moved from beneath her arms down her sides to her waist as he steadied her. The trail his touch left locked her breath in her lungs and her blood raced through her like rivers of fire, igniting deliciously erotic sensations she'd never experienced before. She lifted her head to meet his gaze. "Apparently not." The words were meant to come out cool and firm with a hint of reproach; instead, they came out just above a strangled whisper.

Jess barely heard her response. He was too stunned by his own reaction to the feel of her beneath his hands. He'd expected her to be hard as leather, but she was soft and made him think of silk.

For a long moment, they stood locked in each other's

gazes, each in a state of shock caused by the intensity of the physical reaction they were experiencing.

It was Gwen who broke the heavy silence between them. "Thanks for not letting me fall." She ordered herself to release him and push away, but her body refused to obey. She wanted to be afraid. Fear brought out the survival instinct in her. But there was no fear, only vibrant, exotic emotions.

"You're welcome." Jess knew he'd never seen a pair of more beautiful green eyes or more kissable lips. The woman he was holding was new, someone he'd never met before. And, he wanted to taste her. His head bent slowly downward.

He was going to kiss her! The message blurted loud in Gwen's mind. Flashes of memory pierced her consciousness. Panic filled her as vows she'd made to herself a thousand times echoed in her brain. Sanity returned and, with every fiber of her being, she knew being kissed by Jess Logan could lead her down a path she had sworn never to follow. "No." The word came out roughly, and she pushed at him.

Startled to find a struggling lioness suddenly in his grasp, Jess released her and stepped back. "I wasn't going to do you bodily harm. I was only going to kiss you."

"I don't want to be kissed." She turned her back to him to give herself time to regain her composure.

Jess regarded her worriedly. Her face was ashen and she looked as if she might faint. She was, he realized, terrified. "Sorry. I overstepped my bounds. But for a moment there you didn't look as if you'd mind."

Taking a few deep breaths, Gwen regained her color and her composure and turned back to him. "It was clearly a moment of insanity on both our parts,'' she said levelly.

Jess studied her face. The woman he'd seen moments earlier was gone, hidden away, and the Gwen he knew was back. *Too bad,* he thought regretfully, almost able to visualize the thorny shield she'd again wrapped herself in to keep people at arm's length. ''I'll get you a crate to stand on for mounting.''

''Thanks.'' Trying not to think about what had just occurred, Gwen concentrated on Cantankerous, petting him and apologizing in case her near fall had caused him any discomfort.

He nudged her gently on the shoulder as if to say it was all right. A soft smile spread over her face and a soothing sensation curled through her. The sensation and smile vanished in the next instant as Jess returned and her defenses once again came into action.

When she was mounted, he gave her a few short riding instructions, then they headed out onto the range.

Gwen frowned as she jostled along in the saddle. She was definitely doing something wrong.

''Remember what I told you back at the stables. Get into a rhythm with your legs. Keep your feet firmly in the stirrups and flex your knees in unison with the horse's gait. That'll keep you from bouncing so much,'' Jess said.

''I'm trying,'' she retorted, coming down on the saddle especially hard.

''Ouch,'' he muttered for her. ''Maybe we should turn back before you end up having to stand for your meals for the next week.''

Gwen hated failing, especially at something a great many people seemed to accomplish with ease. ''I'm sure I'll get the hang of it in a minute.'' Sturdying her feet even more firmly in the stirrups, she concentrated on coordinating her body's movements with that of the horse. And, as if this little extra bit of effort was all that was required, her bouncing lessened considerably.

"Looks like you've got it," Jess said with approval.

A glow, as if someone had just pronounced her the most wonderful person in the world, spread through her. Mentally she mocked herself for this extreme reaction to his praise. The man definitely had a disquieting effect on her emotions. Levelly, she said, "Whoever said riding a horse was like sitting in a rocking chair was obviously a couch potato cowboy."

Jess grinned back in agreement, then his expression became solemn. "Look, I'm sorry about what happened back at the stables. Just for a minute there your lips looked so damn kissable, I forgot who they belonged to."

"Consider the incident forgotten." Mentally she patted herself on the back for coming to her senses in time. Clearly, he was already regretting even the thought of almost kissing her.

Jess brought his horse to an easy pace beside hers. He was not normally a prying sort of person, but Gwen's reaction to the near kiss gnawed at him. "I didn't mean to scare you. Most women aren't afraid of a simple kiss."

"I wasn't afraid," she lied, keeping her voice calm and controlled. "I'm just not the kind of woman who kisses every man she sees."

Jess continued to study her. "I can't help suspecting that you've had some trouble with a man in your past. Maybe one who wasn't as polite as me."

Gwen frowned at his persistence. "I've never encountered any man I couldn't handle."

Recalling how she'd "handled" Joe Jackson, Jess mentally mocked himself for thinking she might have been abused. "I've always figured you could take care of yourself."

"Well, you figured right."

For the next hour they rode mostly in silence, stopping every once in a while for Jess to check a section of fence. Periodically they'd come across a small group of cattle, maybe two or three, sometimes five, but never more than a handful.

"I thought you had a large herd," Gwen said.

"We raise free-range cattle here. Takes a lot of acreage per cow. When we get ready to bring them in, we use a helicopter to spot and herd them together."

Gwen suddenly reined Cantankerous to a halt. Standing in her stirrups, she shaded her eyes to better focus on a gathering of what she'd assumed until now were cows in the distance. "Those look like buffalo."

"They are. We're working on getting a herd started."

Reseating herself, she urged Cantankerous forward for a closer look. "They're so ugly, they're fascinating."

Jess caught her reins and brought Cantankerous to a halt. "It's probably not smart to get too close."

One of the beasts turned their way and stared at them as if they were invading its territory. Cantankerous shied sideways. "Obviously Cantankerous agrees with you." Gwen tried steadying the chestnut by rubbing his neck and talking soothingly, but she could sense his muscles tensing. "Okay, boy, let's get out of here," she said, reining him into a gentle turn.

Jess brought his horse around, remaining at her side.

"Smart move. For a minute there I was afraid you'd take my words as a challenge."

She knew her behavior in the past gave him a right to think that. "I might be strong-willed, but I'm not stupid." Keeping her attention forward, she could feel a prickling on her neck that told her he was studying her again.

"You're still bouncing in the saddle a little too much, but you're handling your horse like you've been around one all your life," he said after a short while.

"Clearly, males are males. As long as you set limits and make sure they don't cross them, you get along fine."

"And you never let anyone cross those boundaries?"

"Never."

"No moments of weakness?"

"No."

Recalling their near kiss and her quick return to her insular self, Jess knew she meant what she said. He mentally laughed at himself for experiencing even a momentary attraction to such a cold female. Still, he couldn't entirely vanquish the image of the soft, delectable woman he'd glimpsed and wondered what it would have been like to kiss her. *She's not allowed to come out and play,* he admonished himself. *And curiosity about her could get you a black eye,* he added pushing away any further thoughts about getting closer than five feet to Gwen.

Back at the stables, as she dismounted, Gwen clung to the saddle horn even after her feet touched the ground. Her legs ached and her knees felt as if they were going to give out.

"I shouldn't have kept you out so long," Jess growled.

Her ingrained distrust of men was causing her to wonder if he'd done it on purpose...some sort of I'm-tougher-than-you game. But the self-directed anger in his voice and honest concern on his face told her that he hadn't.

Jess took a step toward her. "Can you walk?"

Easing herself away from Cantankerous, she settled her weight on her legs. They ached but they held her. "Yes, I can walk."

"I'm not normally this inconsiderate." He grimaced at her obvious pain. "Guess I was just so fascinated by your company I lost track of time." This was meant as a jest to lighten the atmosphere. Instead, Jess was surprised by how honest the words felt. He had actually enjoyed being with her. She intrigued him.

She tossed him a disgruntled glance, letting him know she was in no mood for humor. "You were so busy taking care of your ranch, you forgot you had a novice rider with you."

"Could be you're right," he replied, silently chiding himself for still being taunted by the woman he'd glimpsed behind the wall. *If she even really exists.* He was beginning to think that maybe he'd imagined her. Gwen appeared too hard and tough to have that soft a core.

"You men are all alike," she grumbled taking another step and straightening her legs a little more so that she felt more balanced. "All that's important to you is your needs."

"Now that's a pretty mean attitude. I said I was sorry." His manner turned impatient. "I haven't been out with a new rider in a long time."

"Just get out of my way and let me go inside and get into a hot bath." Passing him, she limped out of the barn.

Mentally kicking himself, Jess caught up with her and scooped her up into his arms. "Don't slug me," he commanded curtly. "This is strictly impersonal. I'm just going to carry you inside. I figure I owe you that much."

Gwen started to protest but her physical response to him froze her vocal cords. The muscles of his arms and chest were hard as rocks, yet they created a delicious massaging effect as Jess strode toward the house. A fiery heat spread through her easing her aching muscles and soothing her pain. *If I could package this, I could make a million bucks,* she thought, totally amazed.

Lilly and Morning Hawk met them at the kitchen door.

"What happened?" Lilly asked worriedly.

"Did she fall?" Morning Hawk chimed in. "Should we call a doctor?"

"I'm just stiff from riding too long," Gwen assured them, struggling to sound calm so that Jess would not guess the effect he was having on her.

Both frowned at Jess.

"You should have known better," Morning Hawk berated him.

"I know. I've apologized and now I'm going to carry her to the bathroom so she can soak in a hot bath."

"I can walk from here," Gwen insisted, suddenly embarrassed not to be traveling under her own power. She prided herself on being able to stand, both figuratively and literally, on her own two feet.

Paying her no heed, Jess continued through the

kitchen and down the hall. Coming to a halt at the bathroom door, he stood her on the floor. "I'll wait out here until you get into the tub."

Freed from his touch, Gwen missed the medicinal effect of his arms. Fury at herself kept the anger on her face. "That is really unnecessary."

"You could fall. I'm not leaving until I know you're safely in the tub."

Clamping her mouth shut, she limped into the bathroom, closed the door and locked it.

"Unlock that door," Jess ordered. "If you fall, I don't want to have to break it down."

"I like my privacy," she returned, refusing to obey. She knew, with every fiber of her being, that it was perfectly safe to unlock that door and yet it frightened her to do so. She wanted a strong barrier between herself and Jess.

Jess snarled at the wooden barrier. How could someone who felt so soft in his arms be so infuriatingly mulish? "Did anyone ever tell you that you've got to be one of the most disagreeable people in the world?"

"I've taken care of myself all my life. I don't need anyone looking out for me."

Jess leaned against the opposite wall, still glowering at the door. "I don't know why I'm even showing any concern for her," he grumbled. *Because I feel guilty that she's in the condition she's in,* came the response. Still, he found himself thinking about how comfortable she'd felt in his arms, unexpectedly warm and decidedly feminine. Hearing her undressing, he began to visualize what her body might look like...rounded curves, soft skin. Cursing at the route his mind was taking, he shoved the image from it.

"I'm in the tub," she called out from inside. "You can go now."

Jess heard the water running and told himself to leave. Still, he remained in the hall for a short while longer to reassure himself that she really was fine.

Then silently cursing under his breath at the disturbing disruption she was in his life, he went to clean up.

Chapter Five

"I've never been under the impression that my grandsons are perfect," Morning Hawk said as she, Gwen and Jess sat down to dinner. "But I've never thought of any one of them—" her gaze leveled on Jess "—as being thoughtless of others."

Jess sighed with exaggerated heaviness. "How much more groveling do you want me to do before you stop nagging at me? I've said I'm sorry."

Morning Hawk turned to Gwen. "Do you think he's groveled enough?"

Gwen was suddenly very uncomfortable as her dinner companions both turned their attention to her. She hadn't spoken to Jess since their exchange through the bathroom door and she had planned on not speaking to him for a while longer...not because she was still angry with him, but because his presence had such a disturbing effect on her, she was working on ignoring both it and him. However, to her dismay, she wasn't going to be allowed that route. If she did, she'd look petty. "I suppose he has."

Morning Hawk smiled. "Good. It's not good to eat on a stomach knotted with anger."

"I am truly sorry," Jess apologized again with gruff sincerity. "Are you really feeling better?"

"I'm fine," she assured him, the concern she saw in those dark brown eyes of his seriously threatening the shield she kept around herself. Determinedly, she forced herself to recall the number of times her mother had fallen for a man just because he had "incredible" dark brown eyes and how many times that man had ended up being a one-night stand and, the majority of the time, married to boot. To her relief, those memories helped keep the shield in place.

"I'd ask you what you learned about my grandson today, but I figure I wouldn't want to hear your answer," Morning Hawk said, apparently needing to get a final two cents' worth in before the matter was completely dropped. Then with a shake of her head toward Jess, she added as she turned her attention to her meal, "Anyway, wives always want to feel they've got something they need to work on to make their husbands a bit more civilized."

Deciding that she didn't need to make any response, Gwen concentrated on eating and Jess did the same.

"Figured you were going to work on staying mad at me for a while," Jess said as they cleaned up the dishes.

"No sense in that," Gwen lied, a part of her still wishing she could keep the anger between them as a barrier. "When I leave here in a couple of days, you're history as far as I'm concerned.'' Silently, she wished she were leaving that minute.

"I think I'm a little bit insulted to be that forgettable." He was a lot insulted and that puzzled him. He'd been forgotten by women he'd been somewhat interested in and it hadn't bothered him this much.

"I'm sure you're not going to give it a moment's thought once this is over."

"No, probably not." In fact, he told himself, he'd be glad to see her go. He had enough difficult women in his life. His great-grandmother counted for at least three on her own. He didn't want another.

Finishing with the cleaning up, Gwen reached for the kitchen phone while Jess poured himself a cup of coffee. After dialing her home phone number she punched in the sequence that allowed her to listen to her messages. The blood drained from her face. "No. Oh, no." The words tore from her in a low, disbelieving moan.

Jess, on his way out of the kitchen, looked back. Setting his coffee cup down, he strode toward her. "What's wrong?" he said, placing a hand on her elbow to steady her.

His touch, to her shock, helped to keep the terrible ache inside from consuming her. "I'm fine," she managed to say, as she hung up the phone.

"You don't look fine." He placed a hand around her other arm to continue to keep her from collapsing.

Heat radiated from his hands and she felt the numbness fading and her body strengthening. "I have to go to Lubbock." Urgently, she pulled away from him as tears began streaming down her cheeks.

"What's happened?" Jess demanded, following her out of the kitchen.

"A friend of mine, Henry McBane, is in the hospital." Her chin trembled. "He's...he's..." She couldn't make herself finish.

"He'll be all right," Jess said encouragingly, keeping pace with her. Never in his wildest dreams had he ever imagined Gwen Murphy could be so shaken. Nor had he ever dreamed he could feel such a protectiveness toward her.

Gwen shook her head. "No, he won't." Nausea threatened. "He should have told me."

"Told you what?"

"That he'd had a relapse." She reached her room. Grabbing her purse and keys, she did a quick about-face only to nearly run into Jess.

"You're in no condition to drive. I'll take you there," he said, refusing to move aside and let her pass.

"There's no reason for you to involve yourself. This is personal."

"Friends don't let friends drive when they've been drinking or when they're under emotional stress."

For one brief moment, the thought of having Jess as a friend brought a comforting sense of security. *Never, ever go there,* her inner voice mocked her. If he knew the truth about her family, he'd withdraw that offer in a second. "We're not friends. We're barely acquaintances."

"We'll pretend." His voice held no compromise. "You're in no condition to go anywhere alone. You're shaking like a leaf."

He was right. She tried to steady herself, but the tears only began to flow faster. "I'll return the favor someday," she vowed.

Jess frowned impatiently. "There's no reason for

you to feel obligated. I'm just doing what anyone would do."

"I don't like being indebted to anyone."

"No one gets through this life entirely on their own."

Henry's image suddenly filled her inner vision. He was the only person she'd allowed to get close to her. She choked back a sob. "Could we just get going?"

On the way out, Jess paused to tell Morning Hawk where they were going, then guided Gwen to his sleek, deep-blue Mercedes and opened the passenger door for her.

As he rounded the car, she leaned back in her seat and closed her eyes. Memories of Henry and her, from their childhood to now, played through her mind.

Jess started the car and they took off. "You and this Henry must be pretty close."

"We're not blood kin, but he's like a brother to me. He's the nearest thing to family that I have. I can't believe he tried to handle this on his own."

Jess glanced at her. "Sounds like something you'd try todo."

"I suppose." Her jaw trembled. "But he should have told me. He should have told me."

Jess's brow knitted in concentration. "Henry McBane. That name sounds familiar."

"He was in my grade in school."

"Tall? Short? Heavy? Slim? Dark hair? Light hair? Did he play any sports?"

"Slim, blond hair, no sports." The image of Henry in his youth filled her mind. "When I first met him, he was suffering from malnutrition. His mother had deserted him and his father was a drunkard who spent his money on liquor and felt that a box of cereal and a gallon of milk a week was all Henry needed to survive."

Jess looked shaken. "He could have gotten free lunches at school."

"His father considered that charity and refused to allow Henry to participate in the program. The bastard would rather have seen his son starve."

Jess's jaw tensed. "I wish I'd known. I'd have given him my lunches."

"I took care of him. I used to pack huge meals and give him all of it." Gwen grinned at an old memory. "My mother wondered how I could eat so much and still not gain any weight."

Jess suddenly recalled an image of a dark-haired girl and thin, blond boy sitting in the corner of the playground during recess talking quietly. "So, how'd you and Henry become friends?"

"I don't know. We just did." That was a lie. She remembered the moment very well. And Jess Logan had been there. But he'd forgotten the incident and she didn't feel like reminding him of it.

"So, what's wrong with him?"

"Leukemia. The last time I talked to him, he told me it was still in remission. He must have lied." Gwen's chin trembled again and a fresh stream of tears rolled down her cheeks. She brushed at them with her fists. "I just hope we're not too late."

Jess reached over and rubbed the back of her neck. "We'll get there in time." It was a stupid promise. He couldn't be certain he could keep it and he made it a practice never to promise what he couldn't deliver. Still, wanting to take some of her pain away more than he'd wanted anything in a long time, he heard himself making it anyway. He frowned at the road ahead. Gwen

Murphy was having a very peculiar effect on him…an effect he didn't exactly understand. There was something very different about it from anything any other woman had evoked.

Jess's touch had a startlingly soothing effect, spreading a relaxing warmth through Gwen. Then he returned his hand to the wheel and the chill of dread returned. "I'm sorry for being such a crybaby," she said. "I'm usually able to handle situations much better than this."

"We all have our moments of weakness." How truly glad that he was here to help her through this trauma stunned Jess.

Gwen closed her eyes and again leaned back in her seat. She'd thought she'd steeled herself against letting her emotions take control. *So, no one's perfect.* Giving in to her fear and dread, she let the tears trickle down her cheeks.

By the time they reached the hospital, Gwen had herself under better control. Pausing at the door of Henry's room, she turned to Jess. "I appreciate the ride, but this is private."

He nodded his understanding. "I'll be down the hall in the waiting room."

"Thanks." Steeling herself, Gwen entered the room.

Henry, looked toward her. "Hey, lady."

The tears threatened again. "Why didn't you tell me?" she demanded, approaching the bed in long strides.

"You've seen me through all my other bad times. And I've seen the strain on your face. I didn't want to put you through that again."

He was weaker than she'd ever seen him and she

noted that there was no fight left in his eyes. "I've never minded. We're friends. No, that's wrong. We're more than friends. I've always thought of you as family and I thought you felt the same."

"I do. In fact you're the only one I have who cares about me. I just didn't want to put you through the grief of watching me die."

Gwen wanted to tell him that he wasn't going to die, that she would keep him alive by sheer willpower if necessary. But, she knew that wasn't realistic. "I'm glad you changed your mind."

He tightened one side of his mouth to form an embarrassed grimace. "The truth is, I'm a wimp. I'm scared. I don't want to die alone."

Gwen smiled softly. "If you had, I would never have forgiven you."

Henry smiled back. "You've always come to my rescue when I've been afraid."

Pulling a chair up close to the bed, she seated herself and took his hand in hers. "That's what family is all about…being there for each other."

"I've been remembering how we first met."

Gwen nodded as she too recalled the incident. "It was in fourth grade."

"You were the new girl. Joe Jackson and his gang of bullies were picking on me and you came over and told them to get lost."

"I also recall that they didn't pay much attention to me."

Henry gave her an amused look. "So you put yourself between me and them."

Gwen grimaced as she recalled what happened next. "And that only made them taunt you more."

"Then, you called Joe a big brute with a muscle for

a brain. I thought he was going to slug you and cream me. I was certain we were mincemeat." Henry shook his head at their predicament. "Then Jess Logan came over and shooed them off. No one ever crossed him."

Gwen recalled how, even at that age, Jess had been an imposing figure. "Yeah. No one ever did."

"Must have been all that lawman's blood in him." Henry's brow knitted in a thoughtful way. "It was a surprise when he didn't become a Texas Ranger like his granddad, father and both brothers."

Gwen was stunned by how strong an urge she had to defend Jess's decision. The man didn't need any defense. Henry wasn't being critical. He was just musing. Still, she heard herself saying, "Someone had to run the ranch for his mother."

Henry eyed her narrowly. "I didn't mean anything by what I said. Ranching is a hard business. I give him credit for sticking it out."

Gwen frowned at herself. "I know you didn't mean anything. Don't know why I snapped at you."

Henry continued to regard her thoughtfully. "I always thought you had a crush on him. Was I right?"

"Nope." Gwen saw him raise an eyebrow. She'd never been able to lie successfully to Henry. "All right. So maybe I had a childish one, but I grew up and out of it."

Henry yawned shallowly and closed his eyes.

"You sleep now," Gwen said gently. "I'll be here when you wake up."

Henry opened his eyes. "I'm not sure I'll wake up this time and there's something I want to talk to you about."

"Of course you're going to wake up," Gwen returned curtly, a quaver in her voice destroying the certainty in her words.

Henry smiled at her attempt to be tough. "I've been worrying about you these last few weeks. When I'm gone, you won't have anyone and everyone needs someone. You need to let down your guard. You need to let other people into your life."

Gwen's shoulders squared defensively. "You did and look what happened." Immediately, she regretted her words. The man was dying and she'd opened a tender wound. "I'm sorry. I shouldn't have said that."

Henry squeezed her hand weakly. "It's all right. We've always told each other what we thought. And, you're right in that I went through hell when my marriage ended, but I survived and the truth is I don't regret any of it. To really be alive, a person has to experience love and loss and all the emotions that go with it."

"That's your opinion."

Henry's hold on her hand tightened again. "I just don't want to see you left alone."

"I've always done fine on my own. Don't you worry about me."

Clearly too tired to stay awake any longer, Henry's eyes closed. "But I do, Gwen. I do," he said as he drifted off to sleep.

Tears trickled from Gwen's eyes as she continued to cling to his hand. The thought of him being gone did scare her. She would be totally alone, with no one to care if she lived or died, if she was happy or sad. No one. "I'm a survivor," she murmured under her breath. Her jaw clenched in a hard determined line. "I don't need anyone."

Outside the door of Henry's hospital room, Jess

leaned against the wall, his expression grim with resolve. He hadn't meant to eavesdrop. He'd hung around for a minute or two after she entered the room to make certain she could handle watching a friend die. Then curiosity had won out.

When they'd talked about how they'd become friends, he'd recalled that incident clearly as if it had been carefully stored and was merely waiting to be unlocked. Curious, he'd thought, that he'd recall it so vividly.

When she'd admitted to having had a crush on him, he'd been stunned. Never in his wildest dreams would he have thought that was possible. And, he was flattered. Of course the fact that she'd made it clear that she no longer felt that way, something that was totally obvious, quickly killed that sensation.

But what did remain uppermost in his mind was Henry's assertion that she would be totally alone in the world when he was gone. "And, he's right. No one should be alone," Jess muttered to himself. He would be Gwen's friend, whether she liked it or not. "And eventually she'll get used to the idea." Not wanting her to know that he'd heard what had gone on, he straightened from the wall and headed down the hall.

Gwen woke. Tiredness had overcome her as the night had lengthened into the day. Refusing to leave Henry's bedside, she'd rested her head on the bed so that she could continue to hold his hand and closed her eyes. Immediately, she'd fallen asleep. Now, her back was cramping. Still holding his hand, her eyes half-closed, she straightened and stretched out the pain.

"Hi, sleepyhead," Henry greeted her.

Her eyes focused on him. She was surprised by how calm and at peace he appeared to be. "Hi, yourself."

"Jess Logan was in here a couple of minutes ago to check on you. You didn't tell me the two of you had become friends."

"He's a client, that's all."

"Too bad. He's a good person."

"I'd never fit into his circle."

"I never thought of him as having a *circle*. I've always thought of him as walking to the beat of his own drum."

"Whatever the case, he and I will never be in sync."

"You're a stubborn woman, Gwen." He drew a breath with difficulty. "But you couldn't have been a better sister even if we'd been blood related. I love you."

Tears welled in Gwen's eyes. "I love you, too."

"Goodbye, Gwen. Have a good life."

Henry's eyelids drooped. There was a peaceful expression on his face and he looked as if he were merely drifting off to sleep. Gwen realized the lines on the monitor were slowly becoming straight. An alarm rang shrilly.

"Goodbye, Henry," she said. Tears poured down her cheeks and a terrible aloneness closed in around her.

The nurses came and a doctor. One of the nurses came over and tried to pry her hand from Henry's, but she refused to let go. Someone said something about getting the man in the waiting room and one of the other nurses hurried out of Henry's room. The doctor pronounced Henry dead and stated a time.

Then Jess was there, gently but firmly removing her hand from Henry's and coaxing her to come with him.

In the hall, she came to an abrupt halt. "I can't leave," she managed to choke out between sobs. "There must be arrangements that have to be made."

"Mr. McBane left very specific instructions," one of the nurses said, in soft reassuring tones. She turned her attention to Jess. "The doctor gave you the letter? It explains everything."

Jess nodded. "Come on, Gwen, there's nothing left to do here."

A numbness came over Gwen, the flow of tears stopped and she obeyed. As they pulled out of the parking lot, she started giving Jess directions to her place.

He interrupted. "I'm taking you to Boyd and Katrina's home. They're expecting us."

Her jaw firmed. "No. I don't want a bunch of strangers hovering over me, pretending they care while really thinking about what a nuisance I am and wishing I'd disappear."

Jess frowned at her. "They do care and they wouldn't be wishing you'd disappear."

"They don't know me. They have no reason to care, and I don't need anyone's pity."

"There are people in this world who are honestly willing to help those who are going through a difficult time. My family is like that."

"So I've heard. But I've taken care of myself all my life. I'll be fine. I just want to go home. If you won't take me, then let me out and I'll find my own way."

Jess shook his head at her stubbornness. "All right. Which way?"

Gwen gave him directions. The long day had stretched into dusk as they pulled into the drive of a small house on the outskirts of town.

Jess noted that it was well maintained with flower

gardens along the front and sides. There was a homey, feminine look about it…a gracious welcoming air he'd never detected in Gwen.

Reaching the front door, she turned to him. "Thanks for the ride." Her voice held dismissal. Unlocking the door, she went inside.

Jess followed.

Gwen switched on the lights.

Jess's gaze traveled over his surroundings. The house was tiny. He was in the main living area. To his left was an open doorway and the furnishings in the room told him that was the bedroom. On that same side, a second door opened into a bathroom. Toward the rear was a kitchen.

"It's not a palace, but it's mine and I like it."

Gwen's sharply defensive words cut into Jess's inspection. "It's nice," he said. "Cozy."

She gave him a wry look. "Don't be so shocked. Even wild animals have a nesting instinct."

He grimaced apologetically. "It's just a side of you I've never seen before."

"It's a private side…very private."

"You should let more people see it."

Gwen's features hardened. "If people think there's a weak side to you, they'll try to take advantage of it."

There was the quality of a hard lesson learned in her voice and again Jess's gaze narrowed on her. "So someone did try to take advantage of you."

"They tried. They didn't succeed." Her tone put finality to that subject. "I'm home. I'm fine. Thanks for the lift. Now you can go."

Jess ignored the command in her voice. "Think I'll just hang around. It's been a long night and day for you."

"I don't need you hovering over me like I'm a child. I'm grown-up. I can deal with grief on my own."

"No one should be left to deal with grief on their own." Jess headed to the kitchen. "You want some coffee?"

"No." Too tired to argue with him, Gwen went into the bedroom and closed the door. Leaning against it, she closed her eyes and the image of Henry lying in his hospital bed filled her inner vision. The sense of aloneness once again enveloped her and a chill crept through her. Popping her eyes open, she shed her clothes and went into the bathroom. Suddenly realizing that the door of the bathroom that led to the living room was open, she pushed it closed, locked it, then climbed into the shower. Standing under the hot water, she began to cry once again.

Hearing a door close, Jess came out of the kitchen. Realizing Gwen was taking a shower, he stretched out on the couch and closed his eyes. But he didn't sleep. Instead he listened, making certain she finished her shower safely. It wasn't until he heard her bed squeaking that he allowed himself to doze.

Chapter Six

Gwen woke groggily. Her eyes were tired, swollen and sore from crying and her body felt limp. Forcing herself to a sitting position, she focused on the clock on the bedside table. It was midmorning. Panic washed over her. She had to make sure Henry was being properly taken care of. She could not leave his final rest to strangers.

Combing her hair away from her face with her fingers, she left the bed, pulled on a robe and sluggishly opened her bedroom door. Abruptly, she stopped.

"Morning," Jess said, looking up from the newspaper he was reading.

Gwen stared mutely at the man seated comfortably on her couch. His presence filled the room, but what really stunned her was how naturally he fit into her home. He should have looked out of place there...an intruder who had barged unwelcome into her world.

For a moment, Jess found himself silenced, surprised by the reaction he was having. It was verging on arousal. He'd never considered the possibility she could look that incredibly feminine. Dressed in that old cotton robe that showed more leg than he guessed she was aware of, she looked sexier than any woman in the flimsiest negligee. *That's Gwen Murphy standing there,* he reminded himself abruptly. *She'd rather slug a man than kiss him.* "Would you like some coffee?"

"You're still here," was all Gwen could manage to stammer out.

"I told you I was going to see you through this."

"And I told you that wasn't necessary." Suddenly feeling light-headed, she leaned against the doorway.

Jess reached her in long strides. "You need to eat and drink something," he said, lifting her in his arms. Her robe opened more and, realizing she was wearing little or nothing underneath it, the arousal threatened again.

Gwen saw the lust in his eyes. For a moment an answering lust woke in her. Then, again memories from the past assailed her. Her mother had not been a bad woman. She'd loved Gwen and taken care of her as best she could. But Mary Murphy had been a weak woman. The deep-rooted fear of following in her mother's footsteps swept through her. *Never!* Fury at her momentary weakness gripped her. Snatching at her robe, she pulled it tightly around her, and ordered, "Put me down."

The intensity of her anger startled Jess. He must be crazy to be attracted to her, he thought. Tangling with Gwen would be like tangling with a cougar. He liked his women soft and sweet with just a touch of vinegar. She was nothing but vinegar with a dash of salt thrown in for good measure. "Yes, ma'am." He plopped her into a chair.

The sudden descent caused a fresh rush of dizziness. "Oooh," Gwen moaned.

"Sorry." Feeling guilty for overreacting, Jess ordered himself to behave with good manners and not let the disturbing effect she was continually having on him cause him to act rashly. Heading into the kitchen, he poured her a cup of coffee, added milk and took it to her. "Drink this while I fix you some breakfast."

Gwen stared at the cup. "I suppose you put sugar in this, too," she grumbled.

"Nope just milk. That's the way you had it at the ranch."

She frowned in surprise. "You remembered that?"

"Being observant is what keeps a man alive on the range," he returned and headed back to the kitchen, admitting to himself that he was surprised he'd remembered that small detail. He normally wasn't that observant about what other people ate and drank.

Cereal was all he'd been able to find. He'd considered going out and buying groceries, but he hadn't been able to make himself leave her alone for even a short while. Returning to the living room with the cereal, he handed it to her. "Eat."

She ignored his order, set the bowl aside and started to rise. "I need to call the hospital and find out where Henry is. I know the nurse said he'd made arrangements, but strangers might not care and he could be just lying in the morgue with no one taking care of him."

Jess took a position in front of her blocking her ascent, and picking up the bowl, he again extended it toward her. "I've already called. Henry donated his body to science and the hospital has made all the arrangements necessary to fulfill his wishes. His body is being sent to a teaching hospital. Now eat.''

"He always did like taking care of the details.'' She sank back against the cushions of the chair as loneliness again enveloped her. Henry was gone. Really and truly gone. And there was nothing left for her to do for him.

"Eat,'' Jess ordered. "Or I'll feed you myself.''

Her stomach knotted with hunger and knowing she would be sick if she didn't obey, she took the bowl and began to eat. The food tasted like cardboard, but she managed to get it all down.

"Feeling better?'' Jess asked when she'd finished.

Gwen nodded.

"Then I guess it's time to give you this.'' He extended an envelope toward her. "The doctor gave me this last night. He figured you didn't need any more strain just then.''

Vaguely, Gwen recalled the nurse saying something about a letter. Accepting the envelope, she opened it. After reading the contents, she laid it on the coffee table, rose and went back into her bedroom.

Jess normally didn't make it a habit of prying into other people's affairs, but rationalizing that he'd appointed himself Gwen's friend and she had left the letter lying open, he, too, read it. In it, Henry thanked Gwen for standing by him through thick and thin and repeated that to him she was his only real family. He said he was using this letter to say his goodbye to her and went on to explain that he was donating his body to a teaching hospital. Further, he was very clear that he wanted no funeral or memorial service, no headstone in a cemetery, nothing to mark his passing. He also told her that he'd packed a couple of boxes with personal things he thought she might want and told her to take anything else from his apartment that she could use, after which, she was to call a lawyer named in the letter and turn over the finishing chores of taking care of the estate to him.

Deciding he should check on Gwen, Jess quietly approached the bedroom door and listened. When she'd risen from her chair after reading the letter and walked across the room, her movements had reminded him of a rag doll, dragging itself along by sheer willpower. He'd figured she'd gone back to bed. Sleep was a normal escape from dealing with grief. Instead, he heard her moving around. When her footsteps turned in the direction of the door, he quickly returned to the couch and sat down.

Gwen was dressed when she came out. Without a word to him, she headed to the front door.

"Where are you going?" Jess asked, following her outside.

She stood frowning at his car. "I forgot my car is at your place."

He studied the dazed expression on her face and determined that she was only vaguely aware of her actions. "I'll take you wherever you want to go."

She considered refusing then realized how ridiculous that would be. She had no car. Besides, as much as she prided herself on being able to handle anything on her own, she had to admit she really didn't want to face this task alone. "I have to go by Henry's place and pick up a few things he wants me to have. He never liked loose ends left dangling."

Her paleness frightened him. "Maybe you should wait a day or so. Give yourself time to get over the shock. No use adding to it by facing this part too soon.''

She was tempted to agree, but waiting wouldn't make this any easier. Her jaw hardened with resolve. "No. If you won't take me, then I'll call a taxi."

Jess saw that arguing would do no good. "I'll take you." He opened the passenger door for her and waited as she slowly slid in. Again she reminded him of a rag doll. He reminded himself that she had a core of steel. Still his protective feelings toward her continued to grow.

"I need directions," he coaxed when he started the engine and she remained silent.

Gwen closed her eyes and her brow wrinkled as if what he was requesting was difficult for her to supply. Finally, in a monotone voice, she told him how to get to Henry's place.

When they pulled up in front of the condo, Gwen reached for the door handle, then froze in midmotion. "I can't," she said, in strained tones. "I have my memories. That's all I need or want."

Jess was tempted to take her home immediately, but now that they were here, he knew they had to complete the chore. "If you let the lawyer dispose of what we came to get, you'll regret it. These are things he wanted you to have and, after a while, you'll want them, if for no other reason than that Henry wanted you to have them."

She frowned at him. "You read the letter."

He grimaced self-consciously. "Well, yes. I know it was an invasion of your privacy, but I was worried about you. You didn't look so good."

"I've just lost my best friend. I think it's only natural I'm feeling a little drained," she returned tightly.

"So what's done is done. I apologize." Jess's manner became firm. "But now it's time to take care of this bit of unfinished business. You wait there. There's no reason for you to go in. He said the boxes were marked. I'll find them."

Gwen hesitated, then opened her hand and revealed a key.

Taking it, Jess gave her one last concerned glance as he climbed out of the car. Inside the condo, he found the boxes on the dining room table, neatly packaged and addressed to Gwen. He was carrying the second one out, when a gruff-looking man stepped in front of him.

"Where the hell do you think you're going with that?" the stranger demanded.

"To my car," Jess replied in an easy drawl.

"Think again." The stranger reached for the box. "That's my son's stuff and now it's mine."

"Not this. Henry wanted Gwen to have it. Her name's on the box." Jess's gaze narrowed on the man. "Besides, I was under the impression that Henry was estranged from his family."

"So we haven't been close for a long time. But he's still my blood and that makes me his next of kin."

"Get away!" A female voice cut through the air. "Get away from here! Don't you dare desecrate Henry's home with your presence!"

McBane spun around to see Gwen coming toward him, anger on her face. "What the hell?"

Jess caught Gwen by the wrist before she could move closer. Maintaining his grip on her wrist, Jess set the box down and circled an arm around her waist to hold her more firmly. To McBane, he said, "I suggest you take a hike."

"I'll be in my car watching to make sure you don't take anything else," McBane warned, but his threat was idle and even before the last word was out, he was hurrying away.

Gwen continued to struggle to free herself. "That man needs to be taught a lesson."

"Not today," Jess said firmly.

Suddenly, Gwen went limp. "You're right."

Not totally convinced she had become docile, Jess regarded her sternly. "Are you going to behave if I release you?"

She breathed a resigned sigh. "Yes."

Slowly, making sure she was fully steady on her feet, he freed her and walked her back to his car.

Retrieving the box he'd sat down, Jess put it in the trunk, then opening Gwen's door, he said, "Now that you've gotten your fight back, do you want to go inside and see if there's anything else you want before I lock the place up and call the lawyer?"

Gwen shook her head in the negative. "I suppose I should thank you, but I couldn't stand the thought of that man touching any of Henry's things." The mental image of McBane inside Henry's apartment caused her ire to rise again.

"I understand," Jess said and closed the door.

Back at Gwen's place, Jess placed the call to the lawyer while Gwen stood staring at the boxes.

She broke her silence as he replaced the receiver in its cradle. "I can't open them right now."

Jess nodded. "You've been through enough for to-day. They'll keep."

Gwen began to pace around the room. This was her sanctuary. It had always had a cozy, safe feel to it, but today the walls seemed be closing in on her. For the first time in her life she truly felt like an orphan with no human connection. "I've got to get out here," she muttered and headed to the door.

Jess caught her by the arm. "We should be getting back to the ranch."

His touch had a curiously calming effect. Instead of pulling away, without realizing what she was doing, she gave in to a need for friendly contact and laid the top of her head against his chest. Startled by this act of intimacy, she ordered herself to step away. Instead, she heard herself admitting, "I feel so lost. It's like I have no connection left in this world. I've always been a loner, but I've never felt this alone."

Jess wrapped his arms around her, drawing her closer. "You're not alone. I'm here and I'm going to be your friend."

She was aware of his strength and it sent a thrill through her. Desires she had never dreamed she could feel with such intensity radiated through her body. Shaken, she straightened away from him and tried to push free of his hold.

Jess frowned impatiently. "You don't have to fight me off. I'll release you. I just don't want you losing your balance and falling."

She took a step back as he broke contact. "We'll never be real friends. Right now you're feeling pity for me. But when you get past that, you'll regret ever having made an offer of friendship and realize there is no place for me in your life." This statement was made more to put their situation back in perspective for herself than for him. Her body was still feeling the cravings he'd aroused and she didn't want to allow herself to start having any foolish notions about the two of them not only becoming friends but becoming more than friends. It had been just such foolish notions that had ruined her mother's life.

"You're wrong. Until yesterday, I didn't really know you. Now, I do. And I'm going to make a place in my life for you."

She pictured the disgust that would be on his face should she ever tell him everything about her past and her mother's. Her shoulders squared. "You may think you know me, but you don't."

"Maybe I don't know everything about you, but I'm beginning to know you. You're not the hard-boiled, insular person you've always shown the world."

She gave him a dry look. "Mostly, I am. You've just seen me in one of my weak moments. They don't happen often."

For a long moment, he regarded her narrowly. She'd felt so soft in his arms, he'd had a hard time controlling the urge to kiss her. Now she reminded him of ice. "All right. I'll admit, you're prickly as a cactus, but I'm still going to be your friend."

She regarded him cynically. "I can just hear the howls of laughter when you tell that to the rest of your social circle."

His jaw hardened into a determined line. "What other people think means nothing to me. No one should be alone in the world. Everyone needs someone to look after them."

Now certain that it was pity motivating him, pride glistened in her eyes. "Well, I don't. I'll be just fine on my own. I'm not some dumb stray dog that can't take care of itself."

"I never said you couldn't take care of yourself. But

I'm going to be around to offer you a shoulder to lean on when you need it.''

Her gaze went to his shoulders. They looked so sturdy and inviting, the desire to lay her head against them was strong. *He's feeling sorry for you now. After a while he'll start thinking of you as a nuisance again and regret ever having offered to be your friend. Remember all the men who came in, then just as quickly went out of your mother's life.* ''Thanks but no thanks.'' Her jaw hardened even more. ''Let's get back to the ranch so I can get finished with my part of the game you and your great-grandmother are playing and get back to my real life.''

''Have it your way. But the offer stays open.''

Gwen tossed him a wry glance and headed for the door.

Chapter Seven

As they neared the ranch house, Gwen saw a woman rise from one of the chairs on the porch and watch their approach. Jeanette Harrison's mother had sent her daughter to the best boarding schools in the country, thus limiting Jeanette's contact with the majority of the locals, including Gwen. But Gwen recognized the woman from her many pictures in the society section of the newspaper.

Ignoring Gwen, the willowy, beautiful blonde concentrated on Jess as he parked and climbed out of the car. With a petulant pout on her face, she said, ''Where have you been?'' The expression of someone who had been unjustly mistreated replaced the pout. ''Morning Hawk wouldn't tell me a thing.''

''I thought you were in Paris,'' Jess said in an easy drawl.

Jeanette smiled seductively. ''I was, but I suddenly found myself missing you so much, I caught the Concorde back to the States and hired a private jet to get me here as quickly as possible.''

Gwen caught the quick glance toward her out of the corners of Jeanette's eyes and realized the woman was there to find out why Gwen was at the Logan ranch.

Impatience showed on Jess's face and Gwen knew he'd caught the glance as well. ''There was no reason for you to rush back.''

Dropping the facade of innocence, Jeanette faced him squarely. ''All right. So what is going on here? I got an e-mail from Sally Morris—'' she paused to glance at Gwen, then turned her gaze back to Jess ''—saying that *she'd* moved in under your roof. Sally heard Lilly and Lilly's daughter talking about it at some baseball game Sally's son was playing in.''

''Morning Hawk has employed Gwen to do some work for us.''

''I heard that genealogy story. I could have sworn your great-grandmother could already trace her ancestry back to the stone ages and probably beyond, maybe even to the single-cell stage.''

''There's my father's side of the family.''

Gwen was fascinated by Jess's finesse. He hadn't actually told a lie but was still keeping the story of the genealogy alive. She'd heard that the Logans were honest people. Apparently, Jess took that trait to heart.

On the other hand, one of Gwen's clients, a very gossipy type who moved in the same social circle as Jeanette, had told Gwen stories about the woman that caused Gwen to believe Jeanette would lie at the drop of a hat to get what she wanted. Unexpectedly, the certainty that the woman wasn't good enough for Jess swept through her and a protectiveness toward the man filled her. *Anyone would feel protective toward a man who was being stalked by a predator like Jeanette,* she reasoned. Still, shaken by the strength of her reaction, Gwen chose to flee from this uncomfortable situation. "If you'll excuse me, I've got work to do," she said, quickly continuing into the house.

But just inside, out of the view of the two on the porch, she suddenly came to an abrupt halt and listened. "I can't believe I'm eavesdropping," she chided herself under her breath. Still, she stayed.

"I'm available for dinner tonight," Jeanette said, her voice inviting Jess for a lot more.

"I'm not. I've been honest with you, Jeannie. We had a lot of fun when we were teenagers, but we grew up in two different directions. Our lives don't mesh. You like Paris, Monte Carlo and every other watering hole where the jet set mingles. I like it here."

"I've done a lot of thinking about my life lately and decided that it's time for me to settle down. I want a family and a man I can rely on. And I've chosen you."

"It won't work," Jess stated matter-of-factly.

"I'm going to prove to you that it will," Jeanette purred.

"And she might just succeed, if we don't work fast." Morning Hawk's voice sounded from behind Gwen.

Gwen bit back a strangled cry of surprise. Regaining her composure, she wanted to contradict the woman but she'd seen females like Jeanette work. They could turn any man's head if they put their mind to it. Still, she heard herself saying in Jess's defense, "Jess is a big boy. He can take care of himself."

"Well, I'm determined that he gets a look at the other fish in the sea before she sinks her hooks into him."

"It's always a good idea to consider your choices," Gwen agreed. How much she hated the idea of him being snagged by Jeanette disturbed her. Firmly, she told herself that she'd feel sorry for any man Jeanette married. And she did owe Jess. He'd taken care of her these past two days. And keeping him from getting snagged by Jeanette would definitely repay that debt.

"I'm glad we see eye to eye on that." Morning Hawk smiled warmly and placed an arm around Gwen's waist. "Now, come along. It's always hard to lose a friend. You look pale. Lilly has made a lovely cherry cobbler."

Footfalls on the porch told Gwen that Jess was coming and she definitely didn't want to be found where he might realize she was eavesdropping. "I could use something to eat."

Gwen was seated at the kitchen table staring into an untouched dish of hot cherry cobbler when Jess entered.

"You need to eat," he said, command mingling with coaxing in his voice.

The food smelled wonderful, but Gwen's stomach was still knotted with grief and she was worried she'd get sick if she ate. Tentatively, she took a bite. It was welcomed and she took another.

"I'm sorry about your friend," Lilly said, pausing in her work to momentarily place a comforting hand on Gwen's shoulder.

"Thanks," Gwen acknowledged. The atmosphere in this kitchen was what she'd always imagined being surrounded by a caring family would feel like...warm, cozy, comforting. It was the kind of sensation she had only experienced with Henry, and now he was gone. Her gaze traveled over the three other people in the room and she wished she did belong here, but she didn't.

"I think I'll get back to my computer," she said, rising and exiting the room in long strides.

Alone in her bedroom, she had a firm talk with herself. "They are all good-hearted people," she murmured under her breath, speaking aloud to give her words more validity and strength. "But I don't belong here and when I'm gone, I'll soon be forgotten. So don't go getting soft."

Henry's image came back to haunt her and an incredible tiredness swept over her. Lying down on the bed, she fell asleep.

"Gwen, it's time to wake up." An insistent voice penetrated her sleep-clogged mind.

With a groan of displeasure, she opened her eyes a slit. It was Morning Hawk.

"Come along. Everything is ready."

Gwen frowned in confusion. "Everything?" Her gaze passed Morning Hawk to the landscape beyond the window. The light outside was fading. "I've been asleep for hours. I should have been working."

"No. You needed the rest. But now it's time to rise and bid Henry farewell."

Gwen shifted into a sitting position. "I've already done that."

"No. He has bid you goodbye. The rituals after the death are for the living. It is our way of saying goodbye and wishing them a safe and happy journey to the great beyond."

"Henry didn't want a formal service. I have to respect his wishes."

"Who said anything about a formal service? This is

merely your special goodbye to him with the help of two friends. I'm sure he won't mind. He'll understand that you need this for closure. I won't take no for an answer. You don't need to participate. But I will not let a spirit go to the great beyond without a spoken wish to send him on his way.'' Morning Hawk's manner became stern. ''Now come along. Wash your face and brush your hair. We must hurry before the sun sets.''

Realizing it would be futile to continue to protest, Gwen rose grudgingly.

Jess was waiting for them outside with horses, saddled and ready.

Cantankerous greeted Gwen with a nudge and the friendly contact seemed to ease the pain within.

Jess set down a box beside the horse. ''Time to mount.''

''Are you planning to put my grief out of my mind by paining other quarters?'' she asked dryly.

''This will be a shorter ride,'' he promised. Studying her narrowly, he hesitated. ''You don't look so good.'' He turned to Morning Hawk. ''Maybe we should postpone this until she's more rested.''

The honest concern in his voice caused an intensely comforting warmth to spread through Gwen as if someone had wrapped her in a heavy blanket on a cold day. *This isn't personal with him!* she chided herself. *He's just being kind, doing what he considers his humanitarian duty.* The warmth vanished. ''I'm just fine. Let's get this over with,'' she said, stepping up onto the box and swinging up into the saddle.

As they rode out onto the range, Gwen had to admit that it hadn't seemed right not to have some sort of service to bid Henry goodbye. Still, she felt guilty disobeying his wishes.

They rode to the base of a mesa and dismounted.

"Hope you aren't afraid of heights," Jess said, nodding toward a narrow ledgelike path leading upward.

Gwen eyed the height of the mesa dubiously. "Maybe we should do whatever it is we came to do down here."

"The path cuts into the wall a short way up. It's perfectly safe," Morning Hawk said, already starting up the narrow passage.

"If she can make it, then so can I," Gwen murmured under her breath and followed.

Jess followed her.

About twenty feet up the path narrowed even more. As Morning Hawk turned with her back to the rock and scooted along, Gwen came to a halt. "I've never been good with heights," she confessed.

"We'll turn back. This was supposed to help ease your grief, not scare you to death," Jess said.

Gwen hated looking like a coward in front of him, especially when a woman as ancient as Morning Hawk was continuing without a qualm. Drawing a deep breath, she turned her back to the rock wall. "I'll be fine."

"Take hold of my hand," Jess ordered.

Recalling how unnerving any contact with him had been, Gwen refused. "I'm really all right. I can do this on my own."

"We're going up here to bid a spirit goodbye, I don't want you getting killed on the way." Reaching over Jess closed his hand around hers.

Immediately a heat radiated up Gwen's arm and through her body. Along with it came a sense of safety.

It was as if nothing bad could happen to her as long as he had hold of her. *Thoughts like this will only get you hurt,* she warned herself. Still the sensation lingered. Worried that she might let the effect he was having on her take root deep inside, she quickly continued upward, hoping to break the contact very soon.

And her wish was granted. As Morning Hawk had promised, a short way farther along, the path cut into the mesa so that it was walled on both sides. "I'll be fine now," she said, pulling on her hand.

Jess released her easily.

You see, he had no real desire for any contact. He was just playing the Good Samaritan again, she told herself with cynical satisfaction. But deep inside, she experienced a pang of regret that the contact had been broken. Angry with herself, she forced her mind to concentrate on the climb.

When they reached the flat summit, she saw that someone had gone to a lot of trouble. There was a circle of stones with split logs arranged inside ready to be lit. More firewood was stacked a short distance away. Around the unlit fire were three sleeping bags, a basket and a large jug of water.

"You did well," Morning Hawk said to Jess. "This should keep us comfortable until dawn."

Gwen looked at Jess. "You brought all of this stuff up here?" She kept herself from adding *just for me.* But a feeling of pleasure did sweep through her. Maybe he really did care about her. A curl of excitement wove through her.

"I learned early in life that when Morning Hawk wants something done, it's easier to just go along with her," he replied in an easy drawl.

Silly, silly me, she chided herself, the curl of excite-

ment dying a quick death. He was going along with
this rite in the same vein he was going along with
Morning Hawk's plan to find him a wife…he was simply appeasing his great-grandmother. Realizing that for
a moment she'd almost begun to think like her mother,
letting a small show of kindness get blown all out of
proportion, a chill ran through her.

Morning Hawk motioned her toward the bedrolls and
while they laid them out, Jess started the fire.

"Would you like a sandwich?" the elderly Apache
offered Gwen as they sat down.

Gwen shook her head.

"Then we will begin." Morning Hawk raised her
arms skyward and began to chant. Jess did the same
while Gwen sat mutely. Seeing Morning Hawk per-
forming this ritual seemed in keeping with the
woman's personality. But Gwen had expected Jess to
treat all of this with a dry sense of humor. Instead, he
was as solemn as his great-grandmother.

Morning Hawk paused, her attention turning to
Gwen. "We are asking the spirits to guide your friend's
soul to a safe haven. Don't you wish that for him?"

All of Gwen's thoughts turned to Henry. "Yes. Yes,
I do." She felt ridiculous, but she raised her arms toward the sky and let her mind be filled with her companions' chanting. A calmness came over her for the
first time since Henry's death and as the chanting
ceased and they lowered their arms, she smiled softly.
"Henry would have liked this kind of send-off."

"Tell me about your friend," Morning Hawk en-
couraged.

Gwen hesitated, then began talking slowly about
how they had become like brother and sister, adopting
each other as family. She told about some of the good

times and some of the bad. When she finished, she felt cleansed of the intense, nearly unbearable grief that had blanketed her since his death. In its place was a deep sadness she knew would always linger, but there was the beginning of a peace as well.

Taking Morning Hawk's hands, Gwen gave them a warm squeeze. "Thank you. It seems that you have always come into my life when I had no one else to turn to and made it better."

Jess studied Gwen with surprise. "You and my great-grandmother have a history?"

"We need more wood for the fire," Morning Hawk said, her tone letting Jess know this was not a subject for discussion.

His mouth formed a straight line and for a long moment, it seemed as if he was not going to obey her unspoken command to drop the subject. Then with a shrug, he rose to put more wood on the fire.

Gwen breathed a mental sigh of relief. She couldn't believe she'd made such a slip.

Morning Hawk gave Gwen's hand a squeeze. "The Great Spirit watches over all of us."

As Jess reseated himself, Gwen's stomach growled and she realized that she was hungry...very hungry. "I'll take one of those sandwiches now."

All three ate and Gwen was sure no food had ever tasted so good.

"There is something, an incident, I've been recalling," Jess said as they finished their meal.

Gwen cocked an eyebrow questioningly.

"I recall Joe Jackson's bike being totally dismantled and left in a neatly stacked pile in his driveway. The pieces had been wiped clean of any fingerprints and the culprit or culprits were never uncovered."

Gwen smiled. "He used to wait on the dirt road near the old Granger place and try to run Henry and me down. I suspect he did that to others."

Jess was studying her closely. "But it's my guess that none of the others would have had the nerve to dismantle his bike."

Gwen's smile deepened as she recalled how she and Henry had sneaked out late at night, knowing that neither would be missed by the adults in their households, taken the bike and spent some very happy but nervous hours taking it apart. "Someone had to do something. Henry and I went to his parents, but they claimed we were lying. They said we were jealous of Joe because he had a good home and nice things and we were nothing but unwanted brats, who were probably always getting into trouble and blaming it on others. Guess we just figured that since they already thought we were brats, we'd just prove them right...but we weren't stupid brats. We made sure we didn't get caught."

Jess laughed. "You always hung in the background like a little mouse happy to hide from trouble but I suspected it was you. And, I suspected you had a good reason. You never struck me as the kind who would do something mean just for the heck of it."

Gwen gazed into the fire and frowned thoughtfully. "Too bad Joe never learned his lesson."

"He was too bullheaded. He was bound to bully the wrong person one day. When he did, it cost him his life."

Gwen recalled reading in the newspaper about the bar fight Joe had gotten into. The other man had been smaller, but he'd had a gun and used it.

"It would seem that for 'unwanted brats' you and Henry turned out just fine," Morning Hawk noted.

"Yes, we did," Gwen affirmed.

Jess stretched out on his bedroll. "Think I'll get some sleep."

Gwen's eyes rounded. "We're really going to spend the night up here?"

Jess frowned impatiently. "You didn't think I was going to take you and this stuff back down that path in the dark, did you?"

"I guess that wouldn't be such a good idea," she conceded. Noticing that Morning Hawk was preparing to climb into her sleeping bag, Gwen took off her boots and followed the elderly woman's example. Lying on her back, she gazed up at the star-filled sky. A cool night breeze gently caressed her face and its fresh scent filled her nostrils. It was incredibly peaceful here and yet invigorating at the same time.

"Are you warm enough?" Jess's voice broke into her thoughts.

"Yes," she assured him.

"Then good night," he said and closed his eyes.

Morning Hawk added her good-night and rolled over on her side.

"Good night," Gwen said to them both, her gaze remaining on the star-studded sky. A soft smile spread across her face. Henry would definitely have liked this send-off. Fixing her gaze on the moon, she wished him a final goodbye and closed her eyes.

Chapter Eight

Gwen woke to the smell of bacon sizzling. Stretching lazily, she opened her eyes, then blinked against the sunlight until her eyes adjusted to it. "Guess I overslept," she apologized, squirming into a sitting position.

Jess smiled. "You looked too peaceful to disturb. Besides, I'm in no hurry."

Gwen drew in a deep breath, then exhaled. Even the air smelled soothing. "This is a great place."

"It's a favorite sanctuary for my brothers and me," Jess said. "Since we were children Morning Hawk has brought us up here when she felt we needed time to contemplate our lives. And on occasion, I've come here on my own when I needed to think something out."

Glancing around, Gwen frowned. "Speaking of your great-grandmother, where is she?"

"She and her horse were gone when I woke up. Guess she decided she wanted a softer bed than the ground to sleep on."

The realization that they were alone caused a nervous ripple.

Jess nodded toward the ground beside her. "You won't be needing it, but considering how attached you are to sleeping with a bat, I figured you'd feel safer if you had some kind of wooden log nearby."

Gwen glanced to her side and discovered a sturdy piece of firewood beside her.

Jess dished up the bacon, then broke some eggs into the skillet and began to scramble them.

Watching him, Gwen realized that her nervousness hadn't been born of fear. In fact she felt safe with him, very safe. Her nervousness was born from something else...a womanly heat radiating from within. She cursed silently, wishing he didn't look so masculinely handsome. *Men are nothing but trouble,* she repeated the mantra that brought up images of her past. Usually this was enough to cool any budding female yearnings. This time it had little to no effect. Her gaze traveled along his legs. His jeans were taut against his muscular thighs and her heart began to race and her blood to pound. *Stop it!* she ordered herself and shifted her gaze to the fire. "We should probably hurry back to the ranch, just to make sure Morning Hawk got back safely," she said stiffly.

"I called."

She raised a questioning eyebrow.

"I never go anywhere without my cell phone these days," he responded to the unspoken question.

Nature called and Gwen eased out of her bedroll. "I'm just going over behind that boulder."

Jess watched her out of the corners of his eyes. He'd been aware of her inspection. Being sized up by a woman had never bothered him before, but this time it had been different. Her gaze had felt almost like a physical touch as it traveled along his legs and he'd been close to arousal when she'd suddenly looked away. Now that arousal was threatening again as he watched the sway of her jean-clad hips. "She'd take that log to you, if she knew what you were thinking," he cautioned himself under his breath.

Returning his attention to the eggs just before they began to burn, he dished them up. But as he poured them each a cup of coffee, another thought that had been nagging at the back of his mind returned. And it, combined with that remark about some past history with Morning Hawk, refused to go away. "There's something I've been wondering about," he said, when Gwen returned and they began eating.

She looked up as she forked a bite of egg into her mouth.

"That bat of yours. At the time I didn't think much about it, but I noticed that there's the head of a bear carved into it...identical to the one Morning Hawk carved into the bat she gave me when I was a kid."

Keeping her eyes on her food, Gwen shrugged. "When you've seen one bear head, you've seen them all."

"That's what I told myself at the time. But I've been giving it a little more thought and it seems like a pretty big coincidence that yours reminds me so much of the one she did for me."

"So maybe it was the fad when we were young."

"Nope. I was the only kid on the block with a bat with a totem carved into it...my mother's family totem to be more exact."

Gwen shrugged and kept eating.

"So, where did you get the bat?" Jess persisted,

NO POSTAGE
NECESSARY
IF MAILED
IN THE
UNITED STATES

BUSINESS REPLY MAIL

FIRST-CLASS MAIL   PERMIT NO. 717-003   BUFFALO, NY

POSTAGE WILL BE PAID BY ADDRESSEE

SILHOUETTE READER SERVICE

3010 WALDEN AVE

PO BOX 1867

BUFFALO NY 14240-9952

Get FREE BOOKS and a FREE GIFT when you play the...

LAS VEGAS GAME

Just scratch off the gold box with a coin. Then check below to see the gifts you get! →

YES! I have scratched off the gold Box. Please send me my **2 FREE BOOKS** and **gift for which I qualify.** I understand that I am under no obligation to purchase any books as explained on the back of this card.

315 SDL DUYE   215 SDL DUYU

FIRST NAME   LAST NAME

ADDRESS

APT.#   CITY

STATE/PROV.   ZIP/POSTAL CODE

(S-R-04/03)

7	7	7	Worth TWO FREE BOOKS plus a BONUS Mystery Gift!
🍒	🍒	🍒	Worth TWO FREE BOOKS!
🔔	🔔	♣	TRY AGAIN!

Visit us online at www.eHarlequin.com

Offer limited to one per household and not valid to current Silhouette Romance® subscribers. All orders subject to approval.

determined that now that he'd broached the subject, he wasn't going to drop it easily.

"That was a long time ago." Gwen made it sound as if she couldn't remember.

"You're being evasive and it doesn't become you."

Gwen frowned at him. "I'm eating my breakfast before it gets cold. I suggest you do the same."

She was making it clear that this subject was taboo, but Jess wasn't backing off. Somehow, in the past, she'd had a connection to his family, or more precisely to Morning Hawk. He was certain of it. And he wanted to know what it was. It was time for the direct approach. "Morning Hawk carved that totem in the bat and gave it to you, didn't she?"

Her shoulders stiffened defensively. "My bat is none of your business."

"It is as long as my family is involved."

She frowned at him. "All families have their little secrets from each other. The bat is part of my private life and I intend to keep it private. If your great-grandmother had wanted you to know about it, she would have told you."

Jess shook his head. "You're a strange woman, Gwen Murphy. I've never known any female who was so closemouthed about herself."

She shrugged. "I prefer to think of myself as strongly independent."

"That, too." Deciding this conversation was going nowhere, Jess turned his attention to his food. But he couldn't get the questions out of his head. How and why was she connected to his grandmother? He recalled the overheard conversation between her and Henry in the hospital and ugly thoughts began to torment him.

Setting aside his plate, he took a drink of coffee and again looked at her. "Were you abused as a child?"

She scowled at his persistence. "No."

"Now, why don't I believe that? You won't let anyone get near you. You sleep with a bat under your bed." His tone became coaxing. "I'm going to be your friend whether you like it or not. And as your friend, I'm telling you that keeping that kind of stuff inside will only eat away at you."

Gwen set aside her plate and faced him, impatience etched into her face. "I really don't want to talk about this."

Because she was so adamant, normally he would have respected her wishes. But, although he wasn't certain why, it had become very important to him to know what had happened to her. "But I do."

For a long moment, she sat silently. Telling him the truth could solve a couple of problems. The first was that he'd quit asking questions. The second was that knowing more intimate details about her family would stop him from wanting to be her friend. "All right, I'll tell you about the bat." But even as she uttered these words of surrender, she reconsidered. It was too humiliating. Her jaw firmed. "On the other hand, it's none of your business."

"Nothing you say can shock me," he coaxed.

The intense expression on his face told her that he'd come close to guessing the truth. In fact, it was pretty obvious he was thinking something worse than what had actually happened and that was even more humiliating. Stiffly, she said, "When I was fourteen, my stepfather, at the time, decided he wanted to get intimate with me. I yelled. He covered my mouth, so I kicked him as hard as I could where it really hurts and he let out a huge howl. My mother, who had been sleeping, woke up and came running. I told her he'd tried to molest me. He said I was lying and told her that he'd caught me trying to sneak out in the middle of the night. Since I was still in my nightgown, she didn't believe him. She kicked him out that night.'' Gwen stopped. She'd said enough to let him know that if he was thinking she'd been raped he was wrong and that was all he needed to know.

Mentally, Jess breathed a sigh of relief that the harm done her hadn't been as extensive as he'd thought. Or, had it? Had the stepfather returned? ''That doesn't explain how Morning Hawk came into the picture.''

She glared at him. ''Do you really have to know everything?'' Her tone made this sound more like a dare than a question.

Jess eyed her levelly. ''Everything.''

Her chin hardened with dignity. ''All right. All right,'' she said in clipped tones. ''My mother always had to be in love...had to have a man in her life. Before the divorce was even final, she'd found someone to fill my stepfather's shoes. This guy seemed all right but so had my stepfather. So, the night he moved in, I decided to run away. I didn't want to take the road because I figured they'd find me too easily, so I took off across open range. Since we were living at the old Granger place at the time and I headed west, it turned out to be Logan land I was on. After a couple of hours, I saw a campfire in the distance with a small lean-to nearby. I was making a wide circle around it, when someone placed a hand on my shoulder.'' Gwen grimaced. ''I must have jumped a foot. And I swear my heart actually stopped beating for a moment.''

Jess nodded in understanding. ''Morning Hawk

could always sneak up on a person without them hearing. She used to tell me that a spirit had taught her to walk on the wind. I've never bought that story but on the other hand...'' He left the thought unfinished.

Gwen's voice remained terse. ''At the time, I thought maybe she was a spirit. She'd just seemed to come out of nowhere.'' She shuddered slightly at the memory of her fright. ''Anyway, she took me back to the campfire and got me to tell her my story. Then she convinced me that I was better off at home with a mother who cared about me than I would be out in the world on my own. And she said that if I returned home she would send me something to keep me safe.''

''The bat.''

''The bat.'' Gwen's expression hardened. ''So now you know. I hope that's the end of this subject.''

Jess continued to regard her thoughtfully. ''It's really difficult for you to tell anyone about yourself.''

She scowled at him. ''Anyone would find my childhood difficult to talk about. It's humiliating to admit to my mother's weakness for men.'' She chose not to mention the alcoholism nor the truth about her father. She'd revealed as much as was necessary to satisfy his curiosity and there was no sense in embarrassing herself further.

''You're not responsible for her behavior.''

''A lot of people don't differentiate between the behavior of the parent and the child. They seem to feel that one taints the other.''

''I'm not one of those people.''

''Let's drop this subject.'' Gwen's voice left no room for argument.

Jess could almost see the wall she kept around herself closing in tighter. Being her friend could turn out to be even more of a challenge than he could handle. *No.* The word resounded through his brain. A growing feeling deep inside would not let him give up on her. He would be there for her no matter how hard she tried to push him away. "Guess it's time to finish our breakfast, clean up and head home."

"Sounds like a good plan to me," she replied, turning her full attention to getting off the mesa and back to the ranch.

A while later as they rode back to the ranch, Gwen found herself covertly studying Jess. He hadn't judged her harshly because of her family background. In fact, he didn't seem to think that her mother's behavior left any stain on her.

Inwardly, she frowned at herself. So, maybe he was more open-minded than some people. But, his declaration that he wanted to be her friend remained laughable. She'd never fit in with his crowd. She knew she was as good as any of them, but if they learned about her family history, they'd still stick their noses up as if they smelled something rotten.

And, she reminded herself, she hadn't told Jess everything.

Her jaw clenched. Most important, she didn't need or want him as a friend. This last felt like a lie…a big one. *I'm just feeling lonely because Henry is gone. I'll get over it,* she assured herself.

"You're the quietest woman I've ever known." Jess broke into her thoughts.

"I've never liked small talk. If I have something relevant to say, I say it. Otherwise, I keep my mouth shut."

Jess was certain she was using the silent time between them to reinforce the wall she kept around herself and he refused to give her that luxury. "So let's talk about something relevant. How's your research into my possible future wives going?"

"So far, I haven't turned up any deep, dark secrets."

Jess caught the edge in her voice and regarded her thoughtfully. "But something's bothering you."

That he read her so easily, unnerved her. "Well, yes. The more thought I've given to this situation, the more I dislike it. To you and your grandmother, it's a game. But if you start asking these women out on dates, it won't be a game to them. Someone could get hurt. Most women assume that when a man asks them out, he's honestly considering pursuing a relationship. And, I feel that would be especially true for the women on your list."

"And, like I told you, if I was looking for a wife, they'd be the ones at the top of my list of candidates." Another name…Gwen's name, suddenly flashed into Jess's mind. Was it possible that these feelings of concern and protectiveness he was experiencing toward her were because he was learning to care deeply for her…maybe even falling in love with her? Immediately, he rejected this notion. Being Gwen's friend was one thing. Being her husband was another. He was already living with two difficult women, his great-grandmother and his mother. He didn't need to add a third. However, as hard as he worked at ignoring it, the question about the depth of his feelings for Gwen continued to nag at him.

While Jess's assurance should have made Gwen feel better, instead, it caused a very disquieting sensation…almost a pain deep inside. *Who he marries is of no concern to me.* This felt like a lie. Before she realized what she was thinking, the image of herself and Jess walking down the aisle filled her inner vision. *Don't be stupid,* she admonished herself sternly while her stomach knotted more tightly. "I still don't like being a part of this. It doesn't feel quite ethical."

For a while they rode in silence, then a lazy grin spread over Jess's face. "I've been giving what you said some thought and you could be right. So, I've come up with a solution."

Gwen eyed him suspiciously. "I have the distinct feeling I'm not going to like this."

"You're being paid to be a matchmaker, right?"

"Wrong."

He shook his head at her. "Now, Gwen. What else would you call it? My great-grandmother asked you to find me a wife. Isn't that the description of a matchmaker's job?"

She frowned impatiently. "You know that this is just a game and that I wouldn't have agreed to it if I hadn't believed that."

"But you did agree to it. And, since you're so concerned about someone being hurt, I've come up with a way we can assure that won't happen."

"That first day I was driving up here, I almost turned around and went back home," Gwen grumbled. "Now, I'm certain that I'm going to wish I had." But even as she issued these words, she recalled all the support he'd shown her in the past couple of days, and her truthfulness forced her to add, "Although I am grateful to you. It would have been difficult facing Henry's death alone. I owe you for that." She breathed a resigned sigh. "So what is this idea of yours?"

"You'll go, in turn, to each of the three women I selected, explain that to appease Morning Hawk I am allowing you to act as a matchmaker and set up a date. That way they'll know from the start that this wasn't my idea. And if they don't get angry at me for trying to keep peace in my family and they agree to go along with it, then they'll have passed one of the first tests to prove they really are the sort of woman I'd marry.''

Gwen groaned extra loudly to let him know how much she disliked his plan.

He frowned patronizingly. ''It's a great idea. It takes care of your ethical dilemma. From the start, they'll know what's going on.''

''I just don't like the idea of being that kind of go-between. What if you do marry one of them and it doesn't work out? Then the both of you will blame me.''

''I take responsibility for my own actions.'' His voice took on a plea. ''Look, I'm not interested in leading anyone on or hurting anyone. And this is a reasonable way to do that.''

''Susan, Mary Beth and Brenda should know all the facts up-front,'' Gwen conceded.

''So you'll do it?''

She still didn't like playing this role, but as long as she was involved in this mess, she wanted it to be as fair as possible. ''All right,'' she agreed.

Jess smiled. ''Thanks.''

Gwen cursed silently, as his smile caused her heart to skip a beat. Keeping him outside the wall she kept around herself was becoming more and more difficult. Not only could he warm her with a look, he had come up with a plan to save others any pain or disappointment. The thought that he might be as trustworthy as Henry played through her mind. Abruptly, her cynical side came forward to aid her in keeping her wall in place. Perhaps he had an ulterior motive, it suggested. "I don't suppose you thought up this plan to save your male ego some bruising?"

Jess looked at her questioningly.

"If any of the women turn down a date with you, you can chalk it up to their not being interested in being approached by a matchmaker."

Jess grinned. "I've never considered myself a Casanova. My male ego can withstand their rejection."

Even as her cynical side questioned the honesty of this statement, Gwen turned her gaze away from him as tingles of heat spread through her body. Mentally she cursed his grin for making her feel weak in the knees. "I'll make my first call tomorrow. Who should I start with?"

"Susan."

Gwen pictured him with the slender, pretty redhead on his arm and experienced a coldness in the pit of her stomach. These reactions she was having to Jess were much too disconcerting. *Just get this over and done with and get back to your real life*, she ordered herself. "Susan, it is."

Chapter Nine

It was nearly four the next afternoon when Gwen entered Susan O'Rilley's office.

The tall, pretty redhead rose from her desk and extended her hand across it to Gwen. "I don't believe we've ever met, but I've heard good things about you from Deloras Hudson. You saved her from marrying a gold digger."

Gwen accepted the handshake. "She obviously had suspicions or she wouldn't have hired me."

"True, but he was a charmer and without your research she might have married him in spite of her doubts." Susan waved Gwen into a chair on the opposite side of her desk as she reseated herself.

"I'm glad I was able to help."

Susan's manner became official. "You said you had something you needed to speak to me about."

Gwen had practiced several different approaches on her way here, but, face-to-face with the assistant district attorney, words suddenly failed her.

"Clearly whatever it is, it's important." Susan's tone became coaxing. "I assure you, I will handle it with the strictest confidence."

"I suddenly feel very silly, but I agreed to do this and I can't back out now." Gwen squared her shoulders. "I'm here in the capacity of a matchmaker."

Confusion showed on Susan's face. "Matchmaker. I didn't know there were such people in this country."

"Well, I don't normally function in this capacity. In fact, I never have before and never will in the future." Gwen's tone made her last statement a firm vow.

"So why have you come to see me? Have you uncovered something that worries you about whoever you're making a match for?"

"No." Gwen assumed a more professional air. "It's a long story, but the short version is that I owe Morning Hawk, Jess Logan's great-grandmother, a favor. And she has decided that he should seek a wife so she called me and asked me to help find suitable candidates. Jess was not happy about her interference, but because she can be very insistent, he agreed to appease her by going out with three women he considers wife material. You are one of those women." Gwen braced herself to be laughed out of Susan's office.

But Susan didn't laugh. For a long moment she studied Gwen in a thoughtful silence, then she smiled. "Go out with Jess Logan with matrimony in mind. Now that is intriguing."

"I can't swear that he's really interested in finding a wife. His main purpose is to appease his great-grandmother," Gwen rephrased the situation, wanting to make sure the woman understood the true circumstances.

Susan continued to smile thoughtfully. "If it was

anyone else, I'd call and give him a piece of my mind and tell him never to darken my door again, but Jess Logan is another matter." Her manner became decisive. "He can pick me up for dinner this Saturday at 6:00 p.m. My place. And tell him, I'll expect him in a suit and I want to go someplace where the wine is expensive, the service is good, the food is excellent and there's soft music for dancing. That's a definite necessity...dancing." Susan's voice held a seductive edge as she added, "I've heard he's a very good dancer."

Gwen rose. "I know he'll be pleased you've accepted." As she opened the door to let herself out, she glanced back to see Susan smiling to herself...a smile that reminded Gwen of the cat who ate the canary.

Gwen suddenly found herself disliking Susan O'Rilley. "She's much too pushy," she muttered under her breath, as she drove back to the ranch. "Imagine. Setting the conditions of the date and practically picking the restaurant. And insisting that he spend a small fortune on her."

Another mile down the road, she grudgingly admitted that she would have done the same sort of thing herself, just to be on the safe side. It was always good for a first date to be someplace public and on familiar turf. "But I wouldn't have insisted he spend a huge amount of money on me.

"It'll never work," she concluded. "She's much too domineering and Jess won't stand for being bossed around by a woman, even a gorgeous redhead."

In spite of the assurance in her voice, a twinge of uneasiness wove through her. It was possible Susan would fool him into thinking she was soft and pliable. Many clever people were good at hiding their true selves until they felt they were in control.

"Jess Logan can take care of himself," she growled at the road ahead.

But the image of Susan and Jess together filled her inner vision and a very disquieting sensation took possession of her emotions. "Beetles." Tears of self-directed anger welled in her eyes. She was jealous!

Her jaw tightened until it was painful. "I am not," she declared through clenched teeth. "I am merely concerned for his welfare. He's been kind to me and I don't want to see him hurt." A safe harbor suddenly opened. "He's like a brother to me and I'm feeling sisterly concern."

She drew in a long deep breath and let the air out slowly. She was once again in control. But deep in the recesses of her mind, the suspicion that she was lying to herself lingered. "I am not falling in love with him. That would be even more foolish than anything my mother ever did," she declared and switched on the radio to block out any further disquieting thoughts.

Back at the ranch, Gwen found Jess in his office and passed along Susan's message.

"And now that we've moved into phase two, it's time for me to move back to my place," she said, heading toward the door. "You can give me a call when you want me to set up the next date."

Exiting the study and continuing to her room, she experienced a sudden tremendous surge of depression about leaving and returning to her empty house. "Now that is really crazy," she scolded herself under her breath. She'd always preferred being on her own. She felt safer that way.

"I'm still shaky from Henry's death. It has me thinking strangely," she muttered, beginning to pack.

She had just finished tossing the last of her things in her suitcase when a knock sounded on her door. Before she could respond, Morning Hawk entered.

"You can't leave," the elderly woman stated with authority.

A part of Gwen wanted to say that if Morning Hawk really wanted her to stay, she would. But the part of her that kept her wall secure was the one that responded. "There is no reason for me to remain," she replied calmly but firmly as she closed her suitcase.

Morning Hawk closed the bedroom door and stood in front of it barring Gwen's departure. "You're wrong."

"I can't think of a single reason I need to stay." Gwen guessed Morning Hawk still thought she needed help getting past Henry's death. And, maybe, she could use the companionship. But eventually the Logans would want to get on with their lives, lives that wouldn't include her. Better to leave now than to remain past her welcome.

"You're a matchmaker now. That means you have to keep track of your client and make sure everything is going well."

Gwen frowned at her. "We all know this is a game. You're getting what you want. Jess is dating women who are acceptable wife material. And he's fulfilling his obligation to you, so you won't put him through this again. And maybe he'll even find a wife." This last statement caused that disturbing sensation she was trying to ignore to return.

"But what if you've overlooked something. Because you knew this was a charade, you probably didn't do a thorough check. You will need to go back over your investigation."

Relief spread through her. Morning Hawk had, most likely, hit on what was causing Gwen so much discomfort. It wasn't jealousy. Her subconscious was trying to tell her that she'd missed some vital bit of information about one of the three candidates. "I'll go back over my work at my place."

Morning Hawk continued to block the door. "There's something else."

Here comes the sympathy and the stuff about my needing her and Jess to help me cope with my grief. Gwen stiffened herself against it. Relying on other people for support was always a bad idea. Most people turned out to be as reliable as a rubber crutch. Even Henry, her best friend on this earth, had left her...not by his own choosing, but still he was gone.

"I told Lilly she could have a few days off to visit her sister in Houston. She's been wanting to go and I figured that since you were here, this was a good time."

For a moment Gwen was taken aback. This was an argument she hadn't expected. *Pretty lame,* she thought. "I'm sure you and Jess can get along just fine without me."

"You don't understand. It's ridiculous, but my daughter and granddaughter think I need looking after on nearly an hourly basis. Jess has to run the ranch so he's generally not here during the day. If you leave, they'll think they have to cut their vacation short and come home."

In spite of Morning Hawk's determined independence, Gwen could understand her daughter and granddaughter's concern. Alone here at the ranch all day, the elderly woman might fall or have a stroke or heart attack and not be found for hours. "I'm sure Lilly can reschedule."

"No. I've already told her to go and she's gone. Please, you have to stay." Morning Hawk eyed her with concern. "You and Jess didn't have another spat, did you?"

"No."

"Then there's no reason for you not to stay. Dinner will be on the table in half an hour."

"I didn't…" Before she could finish, Gwen found herself alone as Morning Hawk exited, moving much more swiftly than her age would have had anyone believe she could.

"I didn't say I would stay," Gwen muttered, making her full protest to the empty space in front of her. She turned to pick up her suitcase, then stood indecisively. It wasn't fair to Jess's mother and grandmother to have to cut their vacation short because of Morning Hawk. And she did sort of owe Morning Hawk another favor for helping her bid goodbye to Henry.

With a grudging sigh, she plopped down in the chair by the window. The desire to flee remained strong. The homey atmosphere in this house threatened her determination to remain staunchly independent.

The sound of bootfalls caught her attention. Looking up she saw Jess Logan in her doorway. *And then there's him.* He made her feel… She couldn't choose a word. Uncomfortable one moment and safe the next or both at the same time. And those extreme reactions she was having to him and Susan…she really hated those.

"Morning Hawk told me what she did. I'm sorry she's put you in this position. But she's right about my mother and grandmother coming home if you don't

stay," he said with apology. "She knew Lilly wanted
to go and didn't consider the possibility that you'd feel
your job was done and be leaving as well. I know it's
an inconvenience, but I'd appreciate it if you'd remain
until Lilly gets back."

The distance between them allowed Gwen to view
him from head to foot. He had to be the most masculine
man she'd ever seen. She ordered herself to be indif-
ferent, but heat traveled through her. In a flash, all the
times they'd touched raced through her mind and she
was thankful she was sitting as her knees weakened
and her legs felt like rubber. Her body was craving
him. Terror flowed through her. She wanted to leave
more than she'd ever wanted anything in her life. Still,
she found herself unable to refuse the plea in his soft
brown eyes. "All right. I'll stay," she heard herself
saying.

He studied her thoughtfully for a moment and she
wondered if what was going on inside her had shown
on her face. Then he smiled gratefully. "Thanks," he
said and turned and left.

Once again alone, Gwen had a very sharp talk with
herself. What she was experiencing toward Jess was
lust, nothing more. She'd never had a physical relationship with any man and her hormones were finally
retaliating. Well, they could retaliate all they wanted,
she wasn't giving in to them. She would rather remain
celibate than open herself up to the kind of life her
mother had had.

Gwen had just finished unpacking when she heard
booted footsteps again approaching. They stopped at
her door. *Stay cool,* she ordered herself as she straightened and turned to face Jess. "Yes?"

"It occurs to me that I haven't been out dancing in quite a while. I've cleared some of the furniture out of the middle of the living room and was hoping you'd be my partner for a bit of practice," he finished.

Fear swept through her. She was having a hard enough time keeping her emotions in check. To actually step willingly into his arms was out of the question. "I can't." The words blurted out.

He cocked an eyebrow. "I'm not asking you to jump off a cliff. I'm just asking you help me practice my dancing."

She took a deep, calming breath. "I can't dance," she said in leveler tones, relieved to have an honest excuse.

"Then I'll teach you. It'll be a good way for me to polish up my steps."

Even though he hadn't moved closer, Gwen had to fight to keep herself from taking another step backward. "You really don't want to do that. I'm very clumsy. I tried dancing once and almost lamed my partner."

Jess grinned. "I'll take my chances. Wouldn't want to make a fool of myself with one of the most prominent assistant D.A.s in Lubbock."

It took every ounce of self-control she had to fight the disarming effect his grin was having on her. "You wouldn't want to go to your date with your foot or leg in a cast either."

Challenge flashed in Jess's eyes. "If I didn't know how tough a lady you are, I might start thinking you're afraid to dance with me."

"Don't be ridiculous. I'm just trying to save you from bodily harm."

"I'm willing to risk it. Meet you in the living room

after dinner, which, I was sent to inform you, is on the table now.'' The challenge still in his eyes, he added, ''Would you like for me to ask Morning Hawk to chaperon us?''

Her shoulders straightened. Had she let the effect he had on her show on her face? Well, even though having Morning Hawk around sounded like a great idea, she wasn't going to give him any proof that he unnerved her. Meeting his gaze coolly, she said, ''Why in the world would you want to do that? Unless, of course, you want someone on the spot to repair your injured feet.''

''You're beginning to make me wish I owned some steel-toed boots.'' Standing aside, he waved for her to exit and they walked to the kitchen in silence.

Sitting at the dinner table, Gwen told herself that it was silly to be nervous about dancing with Jess. She'd warned him that she was dangerous. After she'd stepped on his toes a couple of times, he was bound to call it quits.

She had just about convinced herself that the situation was laughable except for the damage he might sustain, when out of the corner of her eye she caught a glimpse of his hands as he reached for a plate of food. Immediately she recalled how large and strong they'd felt when he'd insisted on helping her along the ledge of the mesa. The thought of those callused palms against her skin caused stirrings of sensual excitement.

Her head already lowered over her plate, she pressed the ends of the fingers of her left hand against the middle of her forehead and fought the erotic reaction.

''Are you all right?'' Morning Hawk asked.

''Just a slight headache,'' Gwen lied.

"I hope you're not going to use that as an excuse to avoid helping me with my dancing," Jess said, the hint of a dare in his voice.

For a moment, she considered the possibility. But it was such a lame excuse. *I will not be afraid of him,* she declared. Lifting her head, she smiled. "Of course not. It was just one of those momentary twinges."

He grinned back. "Good."

Gwen was certain she saw a twinkle of amusement in his eyes before he again applied himself to his meal. And again the suspicion that he might have guessed, at least, some of the effect he was having on her tweaked through her mind. *Egotist!* she seethed under her breath. He was probably used to women flaunting themselves at him. She recalled Susan's admission that if it had been anyone else other than Jess who had sent a matchmaker to her, she would have thrown them out of her office.

So, actually, what I am experiencing is simply a normal, healthy female reaction felt by a multitude of women toward a man like Jess Logan. It is nothing of any significance. As long as she didn't pay it any heed, it would eventually disappear like a puff of smoke. Satisfied she was once again in control, she ate.

Chapter Ten

Jess watched Gwen out of the corner of his eye as he chose a disc and placed it into the CD player. He knew he made her uneasy. And, he had a strong suspicion as to why. There had been a definite glint of lust in her eyes during their encounter in her bedroom. That, plus her nervousness and the conversation he'd overheard between her and Henry at the hospital, added up to a possibility that he found... He searched for the right word. *Flattering,* he decided best described it.

In the next instant, he discarded that definition. It was something more than flattering. Intriguing?

That wasn't quite it, either. He recalled the notion of adding her to his list of prospective wives and his rejection of that notion. A little voice warned that getting to know Gwendolen Murphy better could prove to be disastrous to his peace of mind. Still, he could not resist.

As the soft country music filled the room, he approached her, made a sweeping bow, then keeping a foot of space between them, placed one hand on her waist and held the other out for her to place her hand in. Even in this highly formal position, with plenty of distance between them, her body felt rigid beneath his touch. "If you're not careful, you're going to snap right in half or, at least, send a few muscles into spasms."

He felt her draw a deep breath, then her body relaxed somewhat. *From a steel rod, to a sturdy oak.* He expected to be amused. Instead, he was noticing the heat of her hands and the way her breasts rose and fell in the most enticing fashion.

He tried a turn. She stepped on his foot, lost her balance and he tightened his grip on her waist to steady her. Beneath his hand, she felt incredibly soft.

"Sorry," she apologized.

A flush had spread over her face and her near-panicked expression made him want to kiss the tip of her nose and tell her it was all right. Then his gaze wandered to her lips and the desire to taste them grew. For a moment he was certain he saw a responding desire in the depths of those green eyes, then abruptly she jerked her gaze away.

"So what about you and marriage?" he asked.

"What?" Her response was sharp, as if she'd been concentrating so hard on something else that she'd barely heard him.

"I thought a little small talk might help relax you. So what about you and marriage?" He already knew the answer from the overheard conversation at the hospital; still, he was interested.

"I've decided to avoid it all together." Again she stumbled on his foot. "Oops! Sorry."

"That's rather an unusual attitude for a match-maker."

She frowned at him, then set her gaze on his shoulder. "I'm not a matchmaker. In fact, most of the time, I'm a match breaker. People who come to me already have doubts and I either allay them or give them feet."

"Don't any of your clients choose to follow their hearts in spite of what they find out?"

"Once in a while. But there's not too many happy endings in those cases. It's usually some woman who thinks her fiancé might be a philanderer. I find out he is. She confronts him. He vows that after they're married he will be true. It turns out to be an empty vow."

"Back to you." He studied her face as she refused to meet his gaze but continued to stare at his shoulder. "What has you so determined not to enter into the state of matrimony?"

"Some women, even though they know better, always choose badly. I don't want to be one of those."

"You don't strike me as being someone who is easily duped."

"Who knows where love is concerned? Once the heart is set free, it could take anyone on a wayward path."

He heard the hint of pain in her voice. "A person could get the impression that you've followed that path."

Her jaw tensed. "Not me. Not ever. But my mother..." Her mouth clamped shut.

"You're not your mother."

"How do you or I know that?" Her jaw set with resolve, she added, "I'm not willing to take the chance."

She reminded Jess of the women in his family when their minds were made up. To try to dissuade them from their chosen paths was impossible or, if not impossible, required an intense determination to even make them reconsider their course of action.

He frowned at himself. He'd vowed to be her friend. The original purpose for this dancing lesson had grown out of that. He'd thought it would lead to a more relaxed situation between them. They'd laugh and joke about how clumsy both of them were. But he didn't feel like laughing.

Ever since the conversation in her bedroom when he'd detected the hint of lust in her eyes, merely being a friend had been difficult to keep in focus. And the easy way she fit in his hands wasn't helping. Her waist seemed to be just the right size and the curve of her hip was tantalizing. He'd danced with a lot of women but this was the first time the mere feel of one in such an open hold had caused so sensual a reaction.

Again she stumbled and his hand on her waist tightened, causing her curves to be even more pronounced beneath his palm. In spite of his willpower, arousal threatened. That was the last thing he wanted her to witness. Considering her attitude toward men, she was sure to bolt if she knew the effect she was having on him. The moment the song ended, he released her.

"Thanks. That should do it. I don't feel so rusty now," he said with dismissal. Then, quickly turning away, he went to the CD player, keeping his back to her.

He heard her say, "You're welcome." And as he glanced over his shoulder to respond, she was already passing through the doorway into the hall.

But even though she was gone, her presence seemed to linger in the room. Feeling the need for some fresh air to clear his brain, Jess went out to the corral to check on the horses. Leaning on the wooden fence, he attempted to sort through the thoughts muddling his mind.

"Something going on between you and Gwen?" Morning Hawk's voice broke into his thoughts.

He turned to see his great-grandmother approaching the corral. "If it's up to her, the answer is no."

"And if it's up to you?"

"I don't know. I'll admit, I've developed a mighty strong attraction to her. But I'm not sure that it's such a good thing. I was looking for a more domesticated female to latch on to for the long haul."

Morning Hawk regarded him sternly. "She's not the kind of woman you can play with. Make sure you know what you want and that she isn't just a challenge to your male ego before you do any pursuing."

Jess's gaze narrowed on the elderly woman. "You're talking as if she'd be on your list of acceptable wives."

"She's the kind of woman who has real staying power. If she loves you, she'll stand by your side through thick and thin and never waver." Morning Hawk smiled. "That's not to say she won't speak her mind and put you in your place a few times."

Jess continued to study his great-grandmother. "Seems to me you've been giving this a lot of thought."

"I give everything about my family a lot of thought," she replied. Then turned and walked back toward the house.

Jess again leaned on the corral railing. He had some serious thinking to do.

When Jess had chosen to end the lesson, Gwen had mentally breathed a gigantic sigh of relief, and had had to force herself not to run from the living room, but to exit with some semblance of dignity. As she strode down the hall to her room, the imprint of his hand on her waist lingered so intensely it was as if his hold were still there. And the heat his touch had emitted continued to spread through her, igniting embers deep within. He had not called off the lesson a moment too soon, she thought as she reached the door of her sanctuary.

Once inside, she flipped the lock, then plopped herself down in the chair and stared at the wall. Her whole body was trembling with arousal. So this was what desire felt like. She thought she'd experienced it before. Being only human, during her life, she'd been infatuated a couple of times. But those times it had been easy for her to shake off the sensation. This time, however, it had taken every ounce of self-control to keep from tasting the skin on his neck. Her whole body flamed as she considered how it would have felt to have been pressed up against the full length of him.

"Now I understand why cold showers are recommended at times like this," she murmured, the heat causing her body to respond in ways it had never responded before until the womanly core within was to the point it felt as if it were going to explode if it wasn't sated.

"And I understand why women make such stupid mistakes," she added. It was difficult to deny such a craving. In fact, if exposed to it on a daily basis, it could become impossible. Her jaw set itself in a hard line. "For someone other than *me*."

In spite of this forceful, confident statement made to the walls of her room, doubt lingered within. "However, it would be smart to avoid him as much as possible."

But try as she might, she couldn't put out the flames he'd sparked to life. "I definitely need a cold shower," she announced and pushed herself from the chair.

Making sure the coast was clear, she left her room. A few minutes later, she stood under a current of cold water to shock her body back to normal. The many times her mother had been disappointed by the men in her life flashed before Gwen's eyes and that, combined with the chill of the water, worked.

Again confident her world was once again in order, she finished her shower. But before leaving the bathroom, she listened at the door for any movement in the hall, then peeked out before actually exiting.

"No sense in tempting fate," she muttered under her breath, practically jogging to her room. Her confidence in her resistance wasn't as strong as she would have liked, and she wanted a few more hours to work on strengthening it.

As she entered her room, she again bolted the door. Then turning toward the interior. A gasp of shocked surprise issued.

"I didn't mean to frighten you," Jess said, rising from the chair she'd recently occupied.

Gwen pulled her worn terry-cloth robe more tightly around her. "I didn't expect you to be in my room." Mentally she patted herself on the back for managing to keep her voice level and cool. There was even the distinct implication that she considered his presence here as trespassing.

"I apologize." He moved toward the door.

Her body rigid with tension, she took several steps from him toward the far side of the room.

"I didn't come here to do you any harm." He unlocked the door and opened it. "There. Now, if you scream Morning Hawk will come running."

Gwen admitted that it wasn't him she was afraid of. It was herself and the feelings he stirred within her, she feared—and that was even more terrifying. "I want you to leave."

"In a minute. First, I'm curious about something."

"You know everything about me I'm planning to tell you. And anything you want to know about the women I'm investigating can wait until tomorrow."

"This will be painless. I promise."

It was clear he wasn't leaving until his purpose had been fulfilled. "Okay. What are you curious about this time?"

He nodded toward her bed. "Why don't you get your bat out? You need to be, at least, semirelaxed for this."

Yes, the bat. It was a symbol that reminded her of why she shouldn't let him break down her barriers. Willing to grasp at anything that would help hold her resolve in place, she picked it up.

Jess shook his head. "I was hoping you felt safer than that with me."

"I sort of do," she admitted. The sight of him was sending currents of electricity through her. *Why did he have to look so virile?* "But this isn't the most comfortable situation for me. I'm barely clothed and we're practically alone in this house. I've always promised myself I'd be at least cautious under these kinds of conditions. Just think of it as a security blanket."

A hint of amusement flashed in his eyes. "Most women I've known have something soft and cuddly, like a teddy bear, for their 'security blanket.'"

She shrugged. "I'm not like most women."

He grinned openly. "You can say that again."

The playful expression on his face made Gwen's knees weak. Her knuckles whitened on the handle end of the bat as she used the bat for a cane to steady herself. *Get rid of him,* her inner voice ordered. With business crispness, she said, "So what do you want?"

"I was wondering if you had a sense of humor."

"You were wondering if I had a sense of humor so you waited in my room and nearly scared me to death?"

"Scaring you wasn't in my plan." He leaned against the doorjamb, hoping to create a more casual atmosphere between them. "Sorry about that." The soft flow of her curves beneath her robe was enticing. This was probably a very bad idea. But he wasn't ready to turn back now. *Just keep your mind on the business at hand,* he ordered himself.

Gwen felt the embers deep within beginning to ignite once more. Not wanting to take a second cold shower, she mustered as much dismissal in her voice as she could. "I think it would be best if you left."

"In a minute." He straightened. "Do you know how to tell if there's an elephant in your refrigerator?"

She stared at him in a stony silence, willing him to leave.

"Come on. Play along. Do you know how to tell if there's an elephant in your refrigerator?"

Realizing that he wasn't going to go until she responded, she said, "By the peanut butter on his breath?"

"No, by the footprint in the pizza. You can tell if he's in the trunk of your car by the peanut butter on his breath."

She gave him a dry look. "That's your version."

"Well, I'm the one telling the joke."

Cute was never an adjective Gwen had expected to use to describe Jess Logan. But as unbelievable as it seemed, he was looking cuter and cuter by the moment. Even cuddly. Alarms rang violently in her mind. She frowned. "You've told me your joke. Now you can leave."

"Not yet. I have another one."

"Another one? You can't be serious." She fought down a rush of panic. She didn't want him guessing how he was making her feel, and it was getting harder and harder to keep her cool mask in place.

"But I am. How do you keep an elephant from charging?"

Gwen forced herself to concentrate on the joke. "Cut up his credit cards."

"That's one for you. So why do elephants paint their toenails red?"

The image of an elephant with painted toenails brought a half grin. "I have no clue."

"So they can hide in the raspberry patch."

Gwen shook her head at the absurdity of his answer.

"So why did the elephant cross the road?" Jess persisted.

In spite of her desire for him to leave, Gwen found herself getting caught up in the game. "I assume for the same reason the chicken did. To get to the other side."

"Wrong. The elephant crossed the road because it was the chicken's day off."

Gwen frowned. "That's unfair. If the chicken crossed the road to get to the other side, then it should be the same reason for the elephant."

"The elephant would never have crossed the road if it hadn't been the chicken's day off."

Gwen continued to frown. "And how do you figure that?"

"Because elephants don't like to cross roads, especially if they're gravel or asphalt. It's too dangerous. They blend in and the drivers can't see them."

She shook her head at the ridiculousness of his response. "Blend in?"

"Sure those roads are sort of grayish."

Gwen stood looking at him for a long moment, then looked down at her bat. A giggle began deep in her throat and grew to laughter.

"So you like elephant jokes," Jess observed.

Gwen shook her head in the negative. "It's not the jokes. It's the ridiculousness of this situation. You're standing in my doorway telling corny jokes and arguing about the answers while I'm standing here with a bat in my hands."

He shrugged while his grin broadened. "So you're a difficult audience. Every comedian gets one of those once in a while."

He looked so...so...adorable. The temptation to put aside her bat and continue this conversation in a less guarded stance was strong.

"And any good comedian knows to leave his audience laughing." With a wink and nod of his head, Jess stepped back, pulling the door closed between them.

Gwen sank onto the bed, the laughter he had evoked now stilled. In it's place was shock. *Adorable.* She'd actually thought of him as adorable. *And cute.* Even worse, she'd contemplated letting down her guard. Well, it was difficult to think of a man telling elephant jokes as dangerous.

She sobered completely. But he *was* dangerous because he had made her want to let down her guard. And, earlier, he'd made her want to do a great deal more.

Continuing to stare at the door, she admitted that if she ever did consider falling in love, Jess Logan was the kind of man she'd be tempted to let down her guard for. But then her mother had thought that her father was a steadfast, good person. And look what had happened to her. She could still hear her mother saying with a deep, regretful sigh, "I just couldn't resist him. And he seemed so sincere."

Of course, there was one big difference between her father and Jess Logan. All of her mother's friends had known that Gwen's father wasn't a good person and they'd warned her mother to stay away from him. As for the Logans, everyone agreed that they were solid, honest, dependable people. What you saw was what you got.

"Still it would be foolish to let down my guard," she scolded herself sternly. "I'd be thinking in terms of marriage and I don't fit his list. The three women he chose are all educated and from respectable families."

All the while, firmly lecturing herself about not letting down her guard, she prepared for bed.

But as she closed her eyes, Jess's face filled her vision and she again felt his hand on her waist sending warm currents through her. With a groan of frustration, she snuggled into her pillow and went to sleep.

Chapter Eleven

Gwen was sitting on the porch Saturday evening with Morning Hawk when Jess came out dressed for his date. He was wearing a suit and tie and, in place of his worn cowboy boots, his feet were shod in a pair of very expensive, black leather ones.

"You do clean up well." She couldn't believe she'd spoken her thoughts out loud.

Jess grinned. "Thanks. Every once in a while a man's got to knock the dust off and go to town."

Gwen wished he wouldn't grin like that. It made her all weak inside.

Morning Hawk was nodding with approval. "Your lady assistant D.A. should be impressed."

His great-grandmother talking about Susan as if she was already his fiancée turned the weakness inside Gwen to something uncomfortable that carried a harsh chill.

"She's not mine yet," Jess drawled. He glanced down at his suit and the toes of his highly polished boots. "Could be her way of life is a little too fancy for me."

"Every woman likes to go out someplace fancy every once in a while," Morning Hawk returned. "She probably just wanted to see if you knew how to get the dirt out from under your fingernails."

Jess held his hands out toward the women. "Did I do a good enough job?"

Gwen looked at the strong, work-scarred hands and the imprint of the one he'd had on her waist while they danced came back sharply. She thought of that hand on Susan's waist and a hard knot tightened within her. "They'll do," she managed to say levelly while Morning Hawk nodded her approval.

Jess tipped his hat and sauntered off the porch toward his Mercedes.

Watching him go, Gwen hoped he had a rotten time. Instantly angry with herself, she corrected her statement and wished him a good time, but that felt like a lie.

"Shall we go in and watch some television?" Morning Hawk suggested as Jess's car drove away.

"Sure." Anything to put Jess and Susan out of her mind.

But nothing on the screen helped. There was a police drama that caused Susan to keep popping into Gwen's head every time someone mentioned lawyers or the D.A. Then Morning Hawk found a western. Jess's image was so strong, Gwen found herself seeing his face in place of the hero's.

Claiming a headache, she escaped. After taking a shower and climbing into bed, she picked up the book she'd been trying to make herself read for weeks. It was written by a financial consultant and contained in-

formation about how to run a small business more
soundly…more efficient methods of keeping records,
tax deductions many people miss, et cetera. She'd
bought it for a class she'd enrolled in because Henry
thought she should learn more about the fiscal side of
running her business. Luckily a case had come along
one week into the course and she'd had a good excuse
to drop it. "I'd rather be earning real money than worrying about how to organize imaginary funds," she'd
told him. But he'd made her promise to read the text-
book.

So she had tried. And the book had proved to be
useful. It was the perfect sleeping pill. Normally, by
the end of the first page she dozed off. But tonight she
continued to be wide-awake. By chapter two, she was
sitting at her computer making a spreadsheet according
to the author's instructions.

She frowned at herself. This wasn't like her at all.
She had a perfectly good method that used ledgers
which couldn't vanish at a simple misstroke of a key.
"But this will enable me to know exactly what my
funds are at any given moment," she said, continuing
to work busily. An inner voice chided her. She always
knew how she was doing financially at any given moment. Some little compartment in her mind just seemed
to naturally keep track without any effort on her part.

The sound of a car pulling up to the house caused
her to glance at the clock. It was barely midnight. The
hint of a smile played at one corner of her mouth.
Somebody obviously hadn't had a good time. *That
shouldn't make you feel so good*, her little voice berated her. She shrugged. "I knew she wasn't right for
him and I didn't want him making a mistake by thinking she was," she muttered back at it.

Bootfalls coming down the hall caused her to suddenly reach for the light switch. She didn't want him to get the impression she'd been waiting up for him. Then, just as quickly she jerked her hand back. He'd probably already seen the light. Besides, she hadn't been waiting up for him, she'd been working on her finances. *Liar!* her little voice mocked her.

Okay, so maybe she had been killing time until he came home, but as long as she was officially his matchmaker, it was her job to check on him.

A knock sounded on her door.

Making certain her robe was securely fastened, she rose and answered it.

"You busy?" Jess asked, his gaze flitting over her then past her shoulder to the interior of the room.

She'd never been so glad to have a computer screen filled with a spreadsheet. "I was just catching up on some record keeping."

He nodded. "I'm going to get rid of this suit coat and tie, then have a nightcap. And, I'd appreciate it if you'd join me so I can give you a report of my date. I figure that since you're my official matchmaker, you should have one." He grimaced crookedly. "Even more to the point, I want you to pass on the information to Morning Hawk and save me from all the questions she's bound to come up with."

"Sure." As he walked away, Gwen discovered her blood was racing. She'd never wanted to hear a report more. But not in her robe. Just his quick look at her in her nightclothes had made her feel vulnerable...too vulnerable.

When she joined him in the kitchen a few minutes later, she was wearing jeans and a large baggy sweatshirt.

"Beer or soda?" he asked, opening the refrigerator door.

"Soda."

Handing her her drink, he nodded toward the hall. "Let's go into the living room."

His fingers touched hers as she accepted the soda and, as usual, sparks of heat raced through her. "Sure." Quickly, wanting to keep distance between them, she headed out of the kitchen. Reaching the living room, she crossed to one of the large overstuffed chairs, its silhouette visible in the moonlit room. Glad of the shadowy darkness, she hoped he wouldn't flick on a light.

He didn't. Choosing the second overstuffed chair, set at an angle where he could see hers easily, he eased himself down into the cushions, stretched his legs out in front of him and crossed them at the ankles.

Her gaze traveled along his sturdy form. The thought crossed her mind that never in her wildest dreams would she ever have envisioned herself in a darkened living room, past midnight, sitting casually with Jess Logan sharing a drink. And yet, this felt so natural. It was as if they belonged here together. *We don't!* She was only here because she was the pawn in a game he and his great-grandmother were playing. "So, how'd it go?"

The moonlight lit the room just enough to allow her to see the hint of a smile at one corner of his mouth. "You can check Susan off the list."

"Too fancy a lifestyle?"

"Too modern a woman."

Gwen smiled dryly. "Never thought I'd see the day when you were threatened by a 'modern' woman."

"Wouldn't exactly say I was threatened." The smile

on his face broadened. "On the other hand, I guess you could say I was."

Gwen told herself that she knew enough and it was time to drop the subject. Instead she heard herself teasing him just like she would have Henry if he'd made this confession. "What'd she do? Tell you what you should order for dinner and lead when you danced?"

"Nothing so mundane. She suggested we go to her place for a bedroom romp so she could see if we were compatible. She didn't want to waste time on me if I couldn't perform to her satisfaction in bed."

Gwen's eyes rounded. "She said that?"

Jess nodded, then said in a musing tone, "Whatever happened to getting to know a person first? I thought women were real big on wanting men to respect them for their minds before they gave up their bodies."

"Most women are under the impression that men would rather check out their body first. I'm surprised you turned her down." Still, she was glad that he had. *The same as I would be glad if Henry had turned down such an offer,* she told herself. A woman who set sex as her very first priority didn't seem like good wife material to her...too demanding and definitely too macho. She'd want to wear the pants in the family and that wouldn't work for Jess Logan.

He grinned. "It would have been too stressful. I'd have felt like a defendant on trial in her courtroom."

Recalling how easily his touch caused her womanly core to ignite, she found herself thinking that he was much too virile not to pass any woman's test. *Stop that!* she ordered herself as the image of him naked began to take shape in her mind. Glad the room was too dark for him to read anything that might have shown in her eyes, she said in a businesslike voice, "So that takes care of that. Who shall I go see next?"

"Mary Beth."

Gwen experienced a sudden leaden sensation in the pit of her stomach. Of all three women on Jess's list, Mary Beth seemed the most likely to fit what he'd want in a wife. *Good!* her inner voice asserted curtly. *Once he's found a wife, your life can return to normal and he'll no longer be a threat to you.* She sank deeper into her chair. She'd actually admitted that he was a threat. Well, she wasn't dead. She'd just set boundaries she was determined not to cross. That didn't mean her mind couldn't run amuck once in a while. Or her heart. *Not my heart.* Lust was all that was involved and that was only natural. Any red-blooded woman could experience animal magnetism once in a while. "I'll call on Mary Beth tomorrow."

"Set the date up for next weekend. Katrina is coming out tomorrow to spend the day with Morning Hawk so you can have the full day to go into town and arrange things."

Jess continued to sit slouched in his chair, his long legs stretched in front of him, showing no sign that he was ready to end this conversation. Gwen, however, was ready to escape. Sitting here in the dark with him was much too enticing and definitely wearing her nerves. "Since that's settled, I'll be saying goodnight." She eased herself out of her chair, forcing herself to move slowly, nonchalantly.

"Just to satisfy my curiosity…"

Apparently, Jess didn't think their business was complete. Mentally she groaned. Refusing to sink back into the deep cushions for fear the way he made her legs feel weak would cause her to have too much trouble rising a second time, she lightly seated herself on the arm of the large chair. "Yes?"

"Do you think I behaved too old-fashionedly? Would you, as a modern woman, want to check out the compatibility of any male you were considering having a lifetime relationship with?"

"I thought I'd already stated clearly that I have no intention of ever getting married or even being intimately involved with a man." She sounded frigid. Good. Maybe that would stop his inquiries into her personal life.

"Well, just pretend you were considering marriage. Would you want a test run first?"

"I don't pretend about such matters."

"Oh, come on. Hypothetically, what would you do?"

"It's not practical to ask advice from someone who has never seriously considered what you're asking advice about."

He cocked an eyebrow. "You've never, never considered the possibility of getting married or even involved with a man?"

Only with you. Her jaw twitched painfully as this thought flashed into her mind. She had to finish this exchange before something slipped out she really didn't want to reveal. Curtly, she said in clipped tones, "If I ever considered getting married, my decision wouldn't be based on sex. It would be based on much deeper feelings and needs than simply lust."

Jess grinned and eased himself out of his chair. "So you really are old-fashioned at heart." Crossing to her, he cupped her chin in his hand and placed a light kiss on her forehead. "I'm glad to hear that. I feel much safer knowing you're looking after my best interests where women are concerned.''

He'd kissed her. Not with passion but with brotherly gratefulness. Still, her whole body felt as if it'd suddenly turned to jelly. "I'm not looking after your best interests. This is all a game, remember?" she managed to return, surprised she could respond lucidly.

He simply tossed her a final grin and strode out of the room.

Gwen took several deep breaths in an attempt to restore her body's equilibrium. Thank goodness she'd been sitting on the arm of the chair. If she'd been standing, she might have melted into a heap on the floor.

"I will not give in to this," she muttered through clenched teeth. But the shell she kept around herself was beginning to show cracks, very deep cracks. In the next instant she was admitting that if she was to trust a man, Jess Logan would be that man.

"Now you're really getting stupid," she grumbled at herself. He'd never consider her wife material. He'd chosen a lawyer, a teacher and nurse. Sure, she'd managed to acquire her investigator's license and she had a diploma from the local junior college, but the majority of her education had come from the school of hard knocks. "You're getting soft in the head," she finished, pushing herself to a standing position. "Or, more likely, my hormones are trying to take the path my mother's took and look where that led her." This grim reminder of a road she's vowed never to travel helped steel her legs and she strode to her room.

Chapter Twelve

The next morning, Gwen was up and dressed at the crack of dawn. As she hurried down the hall to the kitchen, she could hear water running in the bathroom and knew Jess was in there shaving. *Good.* She needed a day that didn't start with him on the other side of the breakfast table.

"Good morning," she greeted Morning Hawk, not even pausing as she continued to the coffeepot and poured herself a cup. "I have a lot to do in town today, so I'm just going to take my coffee and be on my way."

Morning Hawk eyed her suspiciously. "You remind me of my grandsons when they're trying to get out of the house without telling their mother something she should know. I heard Jess come in and the two of you heading into the living room. Are you trying to get out of the line of fire before he comes in and tells me what he told you?"

"He didn't tell me anything that will disturb you,"

Gwen assured her. Then remembering the reason for her and Jess's late-night conversation, she added, "He's decided that Susan isn't the wife for him. He explained his reasons and I agreed. So we're moving on to Mary Beth."

Morning Hawk nodded as if she'd expected this. "I didn't think Susan would work out."

"So, like I said, I've just got a lot to do," Gwen hurried on. "I figure that since I have to go into town anyway to see Mary Beth, I'll stop by my place, go through my mail and pay my bills." Without giving Morning Hawk a chance to question her further, she left the kitchen by the back door. This way, there was no chance of running into Jess.

But as she drove away from the house, his image was as clear in her mind as if he were there with her. The faint scent of his aftershave even seemed to fill her nostrils. Trying to shake off these disquieting sensations, she concentrated on the personal business awaiting her at home.

A few hours later, her mail was organized, her bills paid and her house cleaned and dusted. Glancing at the clock, she drew a terse breath. She'd phoned Mary Beth earlier and arranged a time to stop by the woman's house. That time was fast approaching.

"I've just never liked Mary Beth," she told the mirror as she finished dressing and gave her hair a final brushing. "She's so...so domestic...so sugary sweet..."

But as she drove toward the woman's house, she forced herself to admit that she'd never felt any dislike toward Mary Beth before now. Her philosophy was that whatever lifestyle made a person happy, as long as it wasn't abusive or destructive, was fine.

Pulling into the driveway of the well-kept split level home, Gwen noted the flower beds were weeded and the blooms on the plants had to be double the size of most. Clearly, the woman had a green thumb.

The door of the house was opened even before she reached the end of the brick walkway.

"I am curious as to why you'd want to come calling on me," Mary Beth said in a genteel Southern drawl, ushering Gwen into the house. Motioning for her to follow, she added, "I hope you don't mind if we talk in the kitchen. I'm baking cookies to freeze for the first day of school. It'll be here before you know it and I like to have a little treat for my students to start the year."

Gwen forced a smile as they continued down the hall and entered a large kitchen filled with the tantalizing aroma of cinnamon, chocolate and peanut butter mingling in the air.

"I always like to make a variety," Mary Beth was saying, indicating the table by the window where a few freshly baked peanut butter and chocolate chip cookies had been set out on a fancy plate. "The first batch of snickerdoodles will be out in about five minutes, if you prefer butter cookies flavored with cinnamon."

"They all look and smell delicious. It's hard to choose," Gwen said politely, seating herself at one of the two spots at the table set out with flowered tea cups and dainty matching plates.

Mary Beth seemed to bubble with joy. "Then I'll just have to give you some of each to take home."

Gwen's stomach was doing flip-flops. "Thanks." It wasn't the cookies. She loved cookies. So what was it?

This kitchen is exactly the kind you think Jess would want his wife to have, her inner voice answered. It was right. She could even visualize him comfortably seated at this table, grinning indulgently at the dainty dishes and telling Mary Beth how great her cookies tasted.

"Coffee or tea?" Mary Beth asked. Her head cocked in motherly fashion, she added, "I'm guessing you're a coffee drinker."

Gwen nodded. She felt as if she'd been mistakenly dumped into one of those family sitcoms where everything came out peaches and cream at the end and all the family members adored each other. This had to be exactly what Jess was looking for. *So good for him. He'll marry her and then I'll be able to get rid of the way he makes me feel and get back to the life I want.*

"So tell me. What has brought you to my door?" Mary Beth said, pouring Gwen a cup of coffee and then seating herself.

"It's rather unusual," Gwen began, wondering how to approach the subject, then deciding that again, the direct route would be the best. "Do you remember Jess Logan?" This was, Gwen thought, a stupid question. Anyone who'd ever come into contact with him would surely remember him. In the next instant, she was mocking herself. She was giving him more credit than he was due. No man was that unforgettable. *Wrong!* The word popped into her mind as Mary Beth's eyes suddenly lit with an appreciative glimmer.

"Of course, I do," the brunette replied. "What red-blooded female from that little community we grew up in wouldn't know who all the Logan men are?" The buzzer on her stove went off and she rose to take care of her cookies.

"Right." The image of feeding Jess to a hungry lioness filled Gwen's inner vision. The urge to leave was strong, but how would she explain that to Jess and Morning Hawk?

Mary Beth set the hot cookies aside to cool, slipped another batch in to cook, then returned to the table. "So what has Jess Logan got to do with your visit to me?"

"His great-grandmother has gotten it into her head that it's time he found a wife and she's hired me to be the matchmaker," Gwen said stiffly.

Mary Beth laughed. "You've got to be kidding. I can't imagine him going along with that."

"You don't know Morning Hawk. Once she's set her mind on something, it's easier to go along with her. Anyway, that's what he's decided to do. He's not seriously looking for a wife, but he has agreed to date a few women we've picked out as possible wives."

Mary Beth was now eyeing her with intense interest. "Really?"

"It's just to appease his grandmother," Gwen said firmly, wanting to make certain Jess's position was stated clearly.

"Yes, of course." Mary Beth was smiling like the cat who'd caught the canary. "Can I assume you're here to set up a date?"

Gwen was puzzled by the woman's behavior. She'd have bet that Mary Beth's first reaction would have been shock that a man would play such a game. "Yes, that is why I'm here."

The woman suddenly frowned. "You don't chaperon, do you?"

"No. You're on your own."

The buzzer on the stove sounded again and Mary Beth nearly danced over to take out the cooked batch.

Not even taking the time to put in a fresh batch, she turned back to Gwen, smiling once again. "So when shall we set this up?"

Did every woman in the county secretly want to date Jess? Gwen mused. *So why wouldn't they?* her little voice mocked the question. He was a hunk. He was wealthy. He was a good man. This last admission shook her as she realized that she truly believed he could be trusted. "Some time this coming weekend."

"Sunday. Yes, Sunday. That would be great. My church is having a social. There'll be a potluck dinner followed by dancing to a country band. He can pick me up at five. I have to help set things up for the dinner and we can always use another pair of strong shoulders around in case we need any tables moved."

"I'll tell him." Gwen rose to leave.

"Oh, you can't go without some cookies. Some for you and some for Jess and his grandmother." Mary Beth flitted around the kitchen getting out bags and filling them. Handing the cookies to Gwen, she grinned widely. "I cannot tell you how much your visit has brightened my day. This will be such fun."

Laden with fresh baked goods, as she reached her car, Gwen glanced over her shoulder to see Mary Beth standing in the doorway of her house still grinning. Continuing to look exceptionally pleased, the brunette waved a cheerful goodbye to Gwen, then went inside as Gwen drove away.

All the way back to the ranch, Mary Beth's excitement and delight taunted Gwen. Maybe, in spite of Gwen's assurances that Jess wasn't really looking for a wife, Mary Beth was feeling confident she could snare him with her cooking and wholesome lifestyle. And, Gwen admitted, maybe she could.

"Nobody can be as sparkling clean as she appears to be," Gwen muttered to herself, deciding that she would take a closer look at Mary Beth Lloyd.

Arriving back at the ranch, she sought out Jess to tell him the date was set. He was in his study going over the ledgers.

"Sounds like fun," he said when she relayed the details. "The food's always good at those kinds of affairs."

"Oh, speaking of food..." She set the largest bag of cookies on his desk. "Mary Beth was baking these and thought you might like a few."

He peered in and issued an appreciative, "Mmm."

Her smile feeling plastic, Gwen made her exit.

"So what do you think of Miss Lloyd as a possible wife for my great-grandson?"

Gwen jerked around to discover Morning Hawk standing a couple of feet down the hall from Jess's study door. "I don't know."

Morning Hawk motioned for Gwen to accompany her and they made their way to the kitchen. There, Morning Hawk poured them both a cup of coffee and nodded toward the table indicating she wanted Gwen to join her. Gwen wasn't in the mood to discuss Mary Beth, but this was, she knew, a command, not an invitation, and seated herself. Realizing she was still holding the bag of cookies Mary Beth had shoved on her, she set them on the table. "These are for you."

"So she's trying to butter up the family as well," Morning Hawk said, peering inside. Getting a plate to put the cookies on, she added, "Obviously an old-fashioned girl. Nice. I like that."

Gwen's plastic smile was beginning to feel as if it

were going to harden into place and she was never going to be able to get the muscles to release. "Yeah, nice."

Morning Hawk had seated herself and was now studying Gwen. "You don't sound convinced."

"She just seems too good to be true." Gwen flushed. "I mean, entering her house is like stepping into one of those fifties sitcoms where the mother was always so perfect and spends all her time tending to her husband and children and keeping peace in the family."

Morning Hawk smiled gently. "And we both know that's not reality, don't we?"

Gwen shrugged. "Maybe. But on the other hand, I'm a cynic. It could be that Mary Beth is exactly what she appears to be…the ideal wife whose entire life would be devoted to her family and home." The words tasted bitter on her tongue as she added, "And that is what Jess is looking for."

"You're right to a certain extent." A male voice sounded from the doorway.

Gwen turned to see Jess enter the kitchen and walk to the refrigerator.

"I do want a wife who's devoted to me and the family I want to have. And I plan to be just as devoted to her," he continued as he poured himself a glass of milk, then leaned against the counter, his gaze on the two women at the table. "But she's also got to have backbone." He grinned at his great-grandmother. "I'm not used to docile women." A gleam of mischief came into his eyes. "'Course I'm not saying I wouldn't enjoy having a woman who'd go out of her way to please me."

I'd be willing to do that. Gwen groaned inwardly as

this admission flashed through her mind. "So maybe Mary Beth will turn out to be perfect for you."

"We'll see. She certainly can cook." Jess left the kitchen, his glass of milk in hand.

"Is something wrong?" Morning Hawk broke the silence that had descended on the room with Jess's exit.

Gwen glanced questioningly at the woman to discover Morning Hawk studying her narrowly.

"You're looking at those cookies as if they were rattlesnakes getting ready to strike," the elderly woman elaborated.

Gwen flushed. "I'm just hoping I'm not a party to getting Jess hooked up with someone who isn't all she seems to be."

"Jess can take care of himself."

"Sometimes, you never discover the real person until it's too late."

Morning Hawk continued to regard her narrowly. "Or maybe you've developed an interest in Jess yourself and you're jealous."

Shaken that the woman had guessed the effect Jess was having on her, Gwen frowned. "Me? That's ridiculous."

"My great-grandson is a good man. I'd think any woman who got to know him would find him real likable. I'm not saying he's perfect, but no man is."

Gwen shrugged with what she hoped was pure nonchalance. "I suppose he's as likable as any cowboy."

Morning Hawk's gaze remained penetrating. "I've caught you looking at him a couple of times with a warm glint in your eyes. And it's occurred to me that maybe you've been thinking that you'd like to be on his list of possible wives."

Gwen was sure of what was coming next. Morning

Hawk had befriended her, but that didn't mean the woman wanted to consider her for membership in their family. Deciding to save them both the embarrassment of Morning Hawk making it clear that she didn't consider Gwen a viable prospect, she said, "That thought has never crossed my mind." Rising from the table, she headed for the door.

"Maybe it should. The Logan men need strong women by their sides."

Gwen froze in her tracks. She hadn't expected that response. Turning back, she met Morning Hawk's gaze. "I doubt the rest of the family would welcome me with open arms. Besides, I'm not interested in a husband. I'm doing just fine on my own."

"You say that like a practiced mantra...something you keep repeating to yourself because you're afraid that if you don't, you might change your mind."

It unnerved her the way the woman seemed to see right through her. "I've got work to do," she said, making a quick escape.

Striding to her room, she locked herself inside, turned on her computer and began to reexamine the data on Mary Beth Lloyd. "I don't want him for myself," she stated curtly to the empty room around her. "But I won't be responsible for him getting hooked up with a phony."

Chapter Thirteen

By the end of the week, Gwen hadn't found out anything disturbing about Mary Beth. The woman honestly seemed to be just what she appeared to be...kind, pleasant, good to animals, children and the elderly.

"A really nice person," Gwen doodled in her notebook while sitting in her favorite café in Lubbock. The establishment was near her place and when she was in town, she was a regular here. It was just past noon on Thursday. Yesterday, Peter Lindsey had called and asked to meet with her and she'd chosen this place and set the time of their appointment for twelve-thirty. At the end of the doodle, Gwen drew a large question mark.

Did Mr. Lindsey have something to tell her that no one else knew about Mary Beth? According to her research he'd dated the woman for nearly two years, but two months ago they'd broken up. She hadn't contacted him because, according to gossip, his mother had been responsible for the breakup and Gwen had no reason not to believe that. Wanda Lindsey was neither pleasant nor nice. For a couple of years, before she'd insisted the family move to Lubbock in spite of the fifty-minute commute her husband would then have to work, Peter had been a classmate of Gwen's and Henry's. He was a quiet boy, painfully shy. She and Henry had considered making him a friend, but his mother had seen them talking after school one day and in a voice so loud that anyone within shouting distance could hear, she'd told Peter that they were not their sort of people and he should avoid them.

Both Gwen and Henry had agreed that they were happy not being her "sort of people" and while they felt sorry for Peter, they'd left him alone. And so had all the other children. Apparently, his mother only approved of a very limited number of playmates for her son and none of them attended public school. Gwen guessed that if the Lindseys had had more money, Peter wouldn't have been in public school either.

"I'm sorry I kept you waiting."

Gwen looked up as a pleasant-faced man, slender and well groomed slid into the seat opposite hers. He glanced at his watch. "I thought you said twelve-thirty. Did I get it wrong? Were we supposed to meet at twelve?"

He was so apologetic and clearly worried he'd been in the wrong, Gwen found herself feeling sorry for him just as she had in grade school. "I said twelve-thirty. I'm early. I had to drop off Morning Hawk, Jess Logan's great-grandmother, at a friend's house for lunch at eleven-thirty, so I just came here right afterward."

He looked very relieved—as if being late would have been a cardinal sin. "I see you already have coffee. Have you ordered lunch? I'm paying.'' He picked up a menu and began reading through it.

Gwen didn't think she'd ever seen anyone trying so hard to be casual. Clearly, he had something very serious on his mind. ''Look, why don't we just talk for a while?''

He laid the menu down. ''I probably didn't have any right to call you.''

''It's a free country.'' He looked so nervous, Gwen began to worry he was going to be ill. Waving the waitress over, she asked for a glass of water for him.

''And I'll have some coffee, too,'' Peter said, obviously feeling he needed to order something immediately to justify his taking up space in the establishment.

''So why did you call?'' Gwen prodded as the waitress hurried away.

''I heard through a mutual friend that Mary Beth is going to our church social with Jess Logan.''

''Yes,'' Gwen confirmed. He looked so uneasy, she wanted to pat him on the hand to comfort him, but didn't. She was fairly certain he wasn't used to people being too familiar with him, especially someone who was barely an acquaintance.

The waitress brought his water and his coffee, refilled Gwen's, then asked if they were ready to order. Gwen asked her to give them a few minutes longer and the woman left.

Peter took a drink of the water, then faced Gwen levelly. ''This mutual friend also told me that Mary Beth said Jess was looking for a wife and you were acting as his matchmaker?''

His intonation made this a question. For a moment, Gwen considered explaining that this was all Morning Hawk's doing, but decided not to. That part was nobody's business but the Logans and the women she contacted. "Yes. That's about it."

Peter's shoulders squared. "I know the Logans have a solid reputation for being decent, honest people. But since Mary Beth doesn't have a father or a brother to look into this matter for her, I feel that I should make certain Jess Logan's intentions are strictly honorable."

"They are definitely honorable," Gwen assured him.

Even though he'd gotten the answer he'd asked for, the man didn't look pleased. "I can't help feeling that she wouldn't fit well into ranch life. She's allergic to horses as well as other animals and she hates the way they smell. And, she's also not fond of dust or people tracking dirt into her house."

"Women have always adjusted to their husband's lifestyle."

"Well, yes."

Gwen noted that his coffee remained untouched while he grew more and more unhappy as their conversation continued. "I'm just going to take a wild stab in the dark and say that I think you still have strong feelings for Mary Beth."

His jaw hardened. "You're right. I do. And I know that if she marries Jess Logan, it will be the biggest mistake of her life."

Immediately, Gwen bristled with indignation. "Jess Logan is a good man," she snapped. She wasn't surprised by her intense defense of Jess. Considering how he'd been affecting her, it seemed almost natural.

"I didn't mean to imply that he isn't," the man said quickly. "I just mean that I feel certain the two of them are not well suited for each other."

Gwen admitted to herself that she felt the same, but she hadn't come up with any legitimate reason to interfere. In fact, until this meeting, she'd been sure that she was letting the way Jess muddled her feelings influence her. However, Peter had just provided her with possible proof that Mary Beth might not be the right woman for Jess.

Resolve etched itself into Peter's face. "I'm going to go have a talk with her."

As displeased as Gwen was with the thought of Mary Beth marrying Jess, she couldn't in good conscience let the woman be dissuaded by a man she considered terrible husband material. "If the gossip is true, you let your mother break the two of you up. No woman needs advice from a man who can't make his own decisions."

"Mary Beth insisted that I choose between her and my family."

"Between her and your mother, you mean," Gwen corrected sternly, certain she was right on this point.

"All right. Between her and my mother. She wanted to get married and start a family. I tried to explain that my mother would never think any woman was good enough for me and I needed more time to convince her that Mary Beth would make a good wife."

"The two of you dated for nearly two years. That should have been long enough."

Peter looked like a man walking barefoot through Hell. "The last time I told Mother I was going to ask Mary Beth to marry me, she had heart palpations. I can't be responsible for her death."

Gwen couldn't help feeling sorry for the man. "It's possible that your mother's heart is as sound as an oak. A faked heart attack is the oldest cliché in the book."

"You could be right. The doctor said he couldn't find anything wrong, but the doctor also said that sometimes it was hard to correctly diagnose such things.'' Peter gritted his teeth. ''I've missed Mary Beth horribly. I do want to marry her, but I can't face the responsibility of possibly killing my mother. She's very high-strung.''

Gwen studied him silently for a long moment. He honestly believed there was a chance his mother would work herself into a heart attack and he could be right. People like Wanda Lindsey could be very destructive to themselves as well as others. An idea began to form. ''What if your mother thought that losing Mary Beth was causing you to plummet to depths that were totally unacceptable?''

Peter eyed her suspiciously. ''What do you mean?''

''As a matchmaker, it's my duty to make certain that the matches I arrange are healthy and viable for both parties. Perhaps I can help you get Mary Beth back in a way that will make your mother both happy and relieved to have the two of you wed.'' Gwen experienced a nudge of guilt. She was offering to help another man win a woman Jess might decide was just right for him. *But, how could someone who is allergic to horses live happily on a ranch?* she reasoned.

Peter frowned. ''You're working for Jess Logan. Why would you want to help me?''

''I've been thinking about what you said about Mary Beth's likes and dislikes, and I have to agree with you that she probably wouldn't like ranch life. So matching her with Jess could be a mistake.''

''It would be a big mistake for her,'' Peter said with assurance.

''Then, I have a plan that could help everyone involved make the correct choice. How about if you take me to the church social? I'm guessing your mother would be appalled that you've stooped to consorting with the likes of me. She might even start thinking that Mary Beth would be good for you, especially if you make her think that you started dating me because you're so desperately lonely and vulnerable since you've broken up with Mary Beth.''

''You really shouldn't put yourself down like that,'' Peter said sincerely. ''I've always admired you and the way you overcame your family problems.''

Gwen shifted uncomfortably. She was fairly certain Peter's mother had been one of the women who had gossiped very loudly about her mother, and Peter had probably been privy to some of the more exaggerated versions of her mother's behavior. ''Thanks.''

Peter extended his hand toward her. ''You've got a date.''

On the way back to the ranch, Gwen told Morning Hawk about her meeting with Peter. ''I realize Mary Beth might be just what Jess is looking for, but I feel I'm doing the right thing. If she is really in love with Peter and marries Jess on the rebound, neither of them will be happy.''

Morning Hawk nodded with approval. ''Good. We would not want to see him making a mistake like that.'' She wrinkled her nose. ''And even if she isn't in love with Peter, her dislike of horses makes her a less than acceptable candidate.''

The guilt that Gwen had been fighting surfaced. ''On the other hand, I might be doing Jess a real disservice. She might be just what he's looking for. She's very domestic and will certainly make her husband and children the very center of her life.''

Morning Hawk regarded her thoughtfully. ''A

woman doesn't have to be the happy homemaker to meet those requirements. I'm sure that if you married, your husband and children would be the center of your life as well.''

Instead of firmly pointing out that she would never find herself in that position, for the first time in her life, Gwen visualized herself as a wife and mother. To her distress, Jess was there. Even worse, a deep yearning to make it all real spread through her. ''Of course they would,'' she heard herself saying, then added dryly, ''but I doubt I'd be as diplomatic as Mary Beth would when they made me angry, and there wouldn't be homemade cookies in the kitchen every day.''

''Jess is used to women speaking their minds openly and clearing the air.''

Gwen glanced at the elderly woman. There was a knowing look on Morning Hawk's face and, again, she had the feeling the woman considered her a candidate for Jess's wife.

Returning her attention to the road, frustration and self-directed anger spread through her. Jess Logan would never consider her viable wife material. If she let Morning Hawk spark fantasies about being his wife, she was sure to get her heart broken. No, her heart was safest locked away and that's where she intended to keep it.

Her jaw firmed with resolve. When this was all over, she would relocate. Colorado was supposed to be a nice place to live. Or maybe Arizona.

As they neared the ranch, Gwen began debating with herself about whether she should tell Jess about her meeting with Peter. The thought of doing anything behind his back displeased her. Deciding that he had to be told, soon after returning, she headed to his study.

"I know this matchmaking business is merely a game to you, but I take my part in it seriously," she began the moment he looked up from the ledger he'd been working on.

"You take everything much too seriously," he returned, giving her his full attention. "So what is the problem now? You told me that you'd explained the situation to Mary Beth."

"I am worried that Mary Beth might be on the rebound." Quickly, she told him about her meeting with Peter. When she finished, Jess was frowning darkly. The fear the he had been seriously considering Mary Beth as wife material and was angry with her for interfering, spread through Gwen.

"I don't like the idea of you placing yourself in the line of Wanda Lindsey's wrath."

A curl of pleasure wove through Gwen. He wasn't angry with her. He was concerned for her. "I'll be fine."

Jess rose and coming around the desk, he placed his hands on her shoulders. "I still don't like it. The woman has a tongue as poisonous as a scorpion's sting."

The protectiveness she read in his eyes coupled with the heat of his touch made her feel as if she were being wrapped in a warm, safe blanket. *Don't overreact,* her inner voice screamed. *He's merely trying to live up to his vow to be your friend.* But even this stern reminder did nothing to dampen the effect. Worried that she might melt into his arms, Gwen took a step back, gently but firmly breaking the contact. "I can handle whatever she dishes out," she assured him.

His renewed protest was cut short by the sound of sharp bootfalls in the hall. In the next instant, Jeanette Harrison entered the study. She tossed Gwen a malicious glance, then turned to Jess with a petulant pout. "I can't believe you lied to me. It's all over town that you've hired *her*..." She paused to point an accusing finger at Gwen for a moment, then returned her gaze to Jess. "You've hired her to act as your matchmaker."

He regarded her levelly. "I never lied to you."

"You said she was here to do some genealogy work for your great-grandmother."

"I never actually said that, I just never denied it."

Jeanette frowned with indulgence. "I guess all men, even you, have their devious side." She smiled seductively. "But I forgive you." Abruptly, her expression became solemn. "And I know that once you've given it some thought you'll forgive me and realize that we belong together." Again she turned to Gwen, this time glaring at her. "You've never liked me. You've always been jealous. I'm sure that when you gave Jess your report on me, you painted my past much blacker than it is." She returned her attention to Jess. "I know I've done a few things you wouldn't approve of, but I was merely sowing my wild oats. What's good for the goose is good for the gander and all that."

"Gwen never gave me any report on you."

"Jess Logan, don't lie to me again. Of course she did. That's why I wasn't at the top of your matchmaking list. You know we belong together."

"I told you before that I'd figured out that we don't," Jess reminded her firmly. "And you know I'm right. I've chosen the life I want and you'd be bored with it in a New York minute."

Jeanette frowned petulantly. "You're wrong. As long as I was with you, I'd be happy anywhere."

Jess regarded her indulgently. "The only reason you're here is that you feel like you've lost something you thought of as yours. You've always been that way." A darkness came into his eyes as if he were thinking of something that greatly bothered him. "Do you remember when our parents wanted us to donate some toys to one of those organizations that fixed them up and gave them to children who had none?"

Jeanette's brow wrinkled in thought, then she said, "No. That must have been a long time ago."

"Well, I do." Jess's voice took on a harsh note. "We were around ten at the time. You threw a fit. And, rather than let someone else have any of your toys, you broke every one of them so badly they couldn't be mended."

Jeanette scowled. "I can't believe you'd remember something like that and hold it against me. I was practically a baby."

"True, but you've never grown out of that bit of spoiled selfishness and I'm willing to bet that you never will."

Jeanette's expression became defiant. "Well, you can believe what you will. And you could be right about us not being made for each other. I certainly never thought of you as being so narrow-minded as to hold a childhood act against me. But I still care about you and don't want to see you doing something that you'll truly regret." Her gaze swung back to Gwen and malice glistened in her eyes. "You want him for yourself. Don't try to deny it. That's why you've been setting him up with women who would never suit him…Susan O'Rilley and Mary Beth Lloyd.'' Jeanette spoke the names with contempt.

Jeanette's gaze jerked back to Jess. ''I'll bet Ms. Murphy's been real careful not to let you find out anything about her past.''

Jess's arm wound protectively around Gwen's shoulders. ''I know all I need to know.''

His action caused a low snarl to issue from Jeanette. ''I knew it. I knew it.'' She smiled acidly at Jess. ''She's totally fooled you. You're so worried about me having one little bitsy bad trait. Well, she's inherited a multitude and they're much worse.''

Gwen guessed what was coming next and stiffened. *This should end any desire by Jess to be my friend.*

Jeannette eyed her challengingly. ''Do you want to tell him or should I?'' Before Gwen could respond, Jeanette decided the issue. ''I'd better, so he gets the full truth.''

''Whatever you have to say is of no importance,'' Jess said curtly.

''It should be. It could even involve the safety of your family. I know I certainly would think twice about allowing anyone with her history to live under my roof.''

''I would never harm Jess or his family,'' Gwen snapped.

''Well, I for one wouldn't take your word for that.''

''I think it's time for you to leave,'' Jess ordered.

For a moment Jeanette looked scared, then her chin jutted out with hateful resolve. ''Her mother told everyone that her father was dead. And she explained the fact that she still had her maiden name by saying that he'd been in the military and killed in a training accident before they could get married. But her story about your father isn't true, is it, Gwen?'' Again before Gwen could speak, Jeanette hurried on. "He never intended to marry your mother. When he found out she was pregnant, he just left...refused to have anything to do with her or you."

"Yes." Gwen's jaw tensed. "My mother never had much luck where men were concerned."

The malice in Jeanette's voice increased. "Do you know what happened to your father?"

"Yes." Gwen had a sick feeling in her stomach.

Jeanette's gaze swung back to Jess. "He died in prison. He was sent there for robbing a bank, got into a fight with another inmate and was stabbed to death. You see what kind of person you have living under your roof."

"My family has always believed that a person is what they make of themselves, not what their parents made of themselves. Now, I'm going to ask you politely to leave. If you don't, I will escort you to the door."

Jeanette stood glaring at both of them for a long moment, then spun on her heels and strode out.

"I'll be packed and out of here within the hour," Gwen said, easing out of Jess's grasp, her face flushed with embarrassment.

He caught her by the arm. "No way are you leaving. I meant what I said. Everything I know about you tells me that you're nothing like your parents." He smiled, tucked his hand under her chin, tilted her face upward and kissed her on the tip of her nose. "We're friends. Nothing's going to change that."

Gwen could barely catch her breath. Terrified that she might make a fool of herself by revealing how deeply she had learned to feel about him, she managed a smile. "I appreciate your confidence in me." Then again gently backing away from his touch, she quickly left the room.

Friendship is all he's offering and all he'll ever offer, she told herself sternly as she continued to her room. Arizona and Colorado were looking better and better with every passing second.

For a long time after Gwen left, Jess stared at the space she'd occupied. *Friends.* That was wrong. He wanted more, much more. He wanted to break down the wall she kept around herself and free the woman he was certain was hiding behind it. "Then..." he muttered aloud.

She'll always be difficult, his inner voice warned, cutting into his train of thought.

I'm used to difficult woman, he countered, his jaw hardening with resolve. He was going to break down that wall.

Chapter Fourteen

Gwen couldn't believe the way she'd behaved about choosing clothes for Sunday night. Her basic wardrobe consisted of jeans and a couple of pants outfits for those instances when jeans weren't quite dressy enough. As for occasions that required something a bit fancier than jeans or slacks, she had a black cocktail dress she'd bought for those once-every-five-years formal affairs and two dresses. The two dresses had been in her closet for as long as she could recall, neither being worn more than two or three times a year.

On Saturday she'd made a quick trip into town to grab one of the two dresses off its hanger for Sunday night. Instead, she'd stood staring at them and suddenly found both of them boring, old-fashioned and dull looking. In the end, she'd purchased a new dress with shoes and a purse to match.

Now standing in front of the mirror in her bedroom at the ranch, she surveyed herself nervously. The dress, a watercolor of pastels, was a sleeveless summer frock with a scoop neck, fitted to the waist with a flowing full skirt that came to just below her knees…modest and yet, with her curvaceous figure, sexy at the same time. Simple pearl earrings, white sandals and a small white purse completed the ensemble.

She was also no longer trying to lie to herself. She'd put this outfit together for Jess.

"You've never wanted to fall in love. And then you go and fall for Jess Logan. You silly, silly woman. There's no future for him and you, and you know it," she mocked the image in front of her. "Worrying about how you look is totally ridiculous." Still, as she jerked her attention away from the mirror and reached for the door knob, she noticed that her hand was shaking.

Continuing to berate herself for letting her emotions rule her brain, she headed for the porch to wait for Peter to arrive.

A low whistle sounded from behind her and she turned to see Jess come out of his office. He looked so incredibly handsome she felt like letting out a wolf whistle herself. It wasn't as if he'd worked hard on his ensemble. He was wearing a pair of slacks, a button-down shirt and Western boots…the usual male garb for a church social. But there was nothing usual about the way he made her heart pound.

"You certainly look nice," he said, his gaze traveling over her thoughtfully.

So do you, she responded silently. Aloud, she said casually, "Figured I'd better try to be presentable. My going with Peter will be a big enough shock to his mother without me showing up in jeans."

His thoughtful expression turned to a frown as a curl of jealousy wove through him. "Looks to me like you've gone the extra mile. I never figured Peter was your type. What happened to the 'I'm never going to let any man get under my skin' woman I know?''

He sounded like an older brother disapproving of her date. She regarded him dryly. ''Peter Lindsey has not gotten under my skin. Like I said, this is strictly to appease his mother.''

''If that's your aim, I'm guessing you've missed it by a mile. Take my word for it, you're going to raise a few eyebrows in that outfit—including Wanda Lindsey's.''

''Well, then that should work even better. I am supposed to be trying to convince Mrs. Lindsey that her son's new choice in women leaves a lot to be desired.''

Jess had to fight the urge to lock her in her room. ''Still looks to me as if you've gone to an awful lot of trouble to help someone you barely know.''

''I'm just trying to look my best,'' she returned with a shrug.

His gaze raked over her again. ''Well, you managed to do that.''

His inspection had a strong masculine edge to it and every fiber of her being flamed to life. ''Thanks,'' she managed to say in a voice that sounded surprisingly calm considering how her body felt.

His gaze traveled over her a final time. She was making him crazy and the patience he'd promise himself that he would exercise was totally unraveling. Turning on his heels he strode down the hall and out the front door.

Gwen stood immobile on the spot where he'd left her. She was certain she'd seen lust in his eyes and it had evoked a responding hunger within her that made her legs weak and her blood run hot. *I would make him a wonderful wife.* The thought filled her mind. *Forget it. You'd never make his list. He'd bed you but he wouldn't wed you.* Drawing a deep breath, she continued down the hall and outside onto the porch to wait for Peter.

Peter, too, had volunteered to show up early at the gathering to help set things up. Thus, he and Gwen arrived at the picnic grounds soon after Jess and Mary Beth.

The brunette was clearly shaken when Peter and Gwen showed up as a pair but either quickly got over it or was able to hide it well. Gwen wasn't certain which.

As they began the preparations, Gwen noticed that the four of them seemed be working as a unit and experienced a twinge of guilt because it was Peter who had managed to maneuver them into this arrangement. However, neither Jess nor Mary Beth seemed to mind, so Gwen chose not to do anything to break up the foursome. She reasoned that this would give Mary Beth a chance to make sure she wasn't still in love with Peter.

And when her conscience reminded her that it was Jess she was supposed to be looking out for, she quelled it by again assuring it that this was exactly what she was doing. He wouldn't be happy married to a woman who was in love with another man.

The band was tuning up their instruments for the dancing later, more and more groups of people were arriving, and the tables were being filled with a delicious variety of home cooking when Gwen felt an icy chill along her spine. Glancing over her shoulder, she saw Wanda Lindsey glaring at her. In spite of the woman's open animosity, Gwen smiled as Wanda approached with her casserole and placed it on the table.

"Evening, Mrs. Lindsey," Jess said with a small, polite bow of his head.

"Jess. Mary Beth. Peter." Mrs. Lindsey said their names by way of greeting. Then, after a perceptible pause, she let herself look Gwen in the face and added an icy "Gwendolen."

"You're looking very nice tonight, Mrs. Lindsey." Mentally, Gwen repeated over and over again in her head that it didn't matter what Wanda Lindsey thought of her. Continuing to smile, she pretended she hadn't noticed Mrs. Lindsey's obvious distaste. Wanda's gaze went to the small bit of cleavage revealed by the scooped neck of Gwen's dress. "I realize you've never had anyone with any taste to guide you in choosing your attire. But really, even a blind person would realize that dress is quite improper for a church social."

"Her attire is much more proper than some that's being worn here," Peter snapped back. "I believe Aunt Jane's daughter left half her dress at home. Maybe you should go talk to your sister about that."

Wanda's attention jerked to her son, her surprise mingled with anger and displeasure. "It would seem your manners have suddenly taken a turn for the worse. Of course, I should have expected that considering the company you're now keeping." Again her gaze rested icily on Gwen; then, uttering "Humph," she strode away.

Mary Beth's eyes rounded in surprise. "I've never heard you speak to your mother like that before," she said. Then, abruptly, she turned her gaze away from him and began to busy herself making certain the dishes of food were arranged properly on the table.

Gwen caught a hint of tears in the other woman's eyes and knew, without any doubt, that Mary Beth was upset because Peter had never defended her so fiercely.

"That old biddy could use a lesson in manners," Jess growled in Gwen's ear.

The protectiveness she heard in his voice took away the sting she'd been hiding behind her polite facade.

"We've worked hard enough. We should get our plates of food and find a table," Peter suggested with authority.

He's certainly feeling good about himself, Gwen noted. Then seeing the water in Mary Beth's eyes continuing to build, she felt a rush of anger. He should have found his gumption sooner.

"You three run along. I'll stay and make sure everything is okay and join you in a few minutes," the brunette said, hurrying away to the dessert table as if her assistance were in demand there.

"I'll help Mary Beth," Gwen said. "You two get your food and find a table." Her tone made this an order and the men obeyed as she hurried after the other woman.

Mary Beth passed the dessert table and headed to a large old oak in the distance.

Gwen caught up with her as Mary Beth stepped behind the oak, out of view of the rest of those gathered for the picnic, and covered her face with her hands.

"Peter didn't defend me because he has any feelings for me," Gwen said, laying a comforting hand on the woman's arm.

Mary Beth uncovered her face to expose streams of tears running down her cheeks. "Don't lie to me. He never faced up to his mother like that when we were dating. You've obviously brought out the man in him like I never could.''

"He's here with me tonight because he doesn't want to lose you."

Mary Beth frowned in disbelief.

"He heard about me acting as matchmaker for Jess Logan and arranged to meet me for lunch on the pretense of making certain Jess had only noble intentions toward you. I could tell he still cared for you and eventually he admitted it. He also told me how his mother had nearly had a heart attack when he tried to face her down over you. It's my guess she was faking it, but he was convinced it was real.''

Mary Beth nodded. "She's used that same ploy before to get her way. I'm surprised she didn't collapse on the spot when he talked back to her just now."

"I think his inviting me has her so unnerved she's worried that her old ploys might not work." Gwen smiled. "Which is working out even better than we planned."

"You planned?"

"I figured that if Wanda saw Peter with me, she might start thinking that having you as a daughter-in-law would be terrific."

Mary Beth frowned. "Am I the only one who doesn't know about this?"

"Jess knows that Peter is still in love with you. I felt that as his matchmaker I should make certain you weren't still in love with Peter. It would be bad business if I let a client marry someone who was in love with someone else. And if in the process of my discovering the truth I made it easier for you and Peter to have a life together, then so much for the better.''

Mary Beth wiped her cheeks. "We should be getting back to our dates."

"Yes, we should."

"I think it would be a good idea if I didn't pay too much attention to Peter. We don't want his mother to think that this was a setup. She should have to believe that Peter had to win me back from Jess."

"Just so Jess doesn't think he's won you," Gwen cautioned, suddenly worried that Jess might start thinking that he and Mary Beth would be a good match.

Mary Beth smiled. "I'll tell him that I'm in love with Peter and ask him if he'll play along to convince Peter's mother that Peter will have to battle to get me back." Abruptly, she frowned. "But I don't think we should let Peter in on this just yet. He deserves to suffer a bit."

Gwen wanted to say that she thought Peter deserved to suffer a great deal, but then recalled the quiet, nearly friendless boy in grade school and simply nodded her agreement.

When they rejoined the men, Mary Beth was her usual good-natured self. "I forgot something in the car," she said to Jess before she sat down. "Would you mind walking me there to get it?"

Jess rose from the table. "It'd be my pleasure."

Peter watched them leave with a worried frown, then turned to Gwen and leaned close. "It has occurred to me that given her other reactions to lesser transgressions of mine, my mother should be in an ambulance on her way to the hospital in critical condition. In fact, the only reason I didn't cancel our date was that I knew at least two doctors would be here and I'm desperate. But look at her. I don't think I've seen her more healthy."

Following his line of vision, Gwen saw Wanda with her circle of ladies, speaking adamantly and periodically glancing in their direction. "Obviously the thought of you with me has had miraculous healing powers on her."

Getting no response, she looked back at Peter to see that his attention had shifted to Mary Beth and Jess who were returning. Mary Beth's arm was hooked through Jess's and the two were laughing.

"I've lost her," Peter moaned under his breath.

"Don't be a wimp," Gwen growled at him. "You've faced down your mother. Surely, Jess Logan can't be much of a challenge after that?"

He looked at her as if she'd lost her mind. "All the Logans have always been considered prize catches."

He was right about that. And when Jess smiled he could touch any woman's heart, Gwen thought. But not Mary Beth's. Her heart was already taken and it was up to Gwen to see that the right match was made. "Well, that may be so, but that doesn't mean that he's the right husband for Mary Beth. In spite of your behavior, she might still be in love with you. Some women are like that. Their love runs deep. You wouldn't want her marrying Jess on the rebound or just because she's angry with you."

"That would be disaster for both of them," he admitted. His shoulders straightened. "You're right. It's up to me to make sure she doesn't make a mistake that she'll regret the rest of her life."

"That's the spirit," Gwen returned encouragingly.

Peter barely heard her. He was already on his feet, heading toward the returning couple to offer assistance to Mary Beth should she need it. When she asked for some iced tea, he was off at a run for the drink table totally forgetting to ask Gwen if she wanted anything more.

"It would seem Peter is trying to impress my date," Jess said with a conspiratorial grin as he and Mary Beth reseated themselves at the table.

"Just don't let his mother catch on to what's going on," Gwen cautioned. "The more worried she becomes about Peter ending up with me, the easier Mary Beth's life as Peter's wife will be."

Mary Beth eyed her hopefully. "Then he really does want me back."

"He's scared silly that you'll fall for Jess."

Mary Beth smiled warmly at the cowboy beside her. "I'm allergic to horses and have never wanted to spend even a minute living on a ranch, but if my heart wasn't already taken, I'm sure you could charm me into accepting a place in your life. I'm sure you could charm any woman."

Jess's gaze fell on Gwen. "Some women are more immune than others."

Wishing she were as immune as he thought she was, Gwen avoided his gaze and was grateful when Peter returned to the table.

"Have you read any good books you could recommend?" Peter asked, as he seated himself, his full attention on Mary Beth.

"A couple," she replied, adding the names and authors.

Peter smiled. "Thanks. I can always count on you to recommend books I'll enjoy."

"You wouldn't be flirting with my date, would you?" Jess asked in an easy drawl, lacing his voice with a hint of intimidation.

Peter's shoulders straightened. "I'm merely making

conversation.'' His chin stiffened. ''Besides, it's not like she's your property.''

''I'm nobody's property, nor will I ever be anybody's *property*,'' Mary Beth said in a quiet but firm voice.

Peter flushed. ''I didn't mean to imply that you would ever be anything but an equal partner in any relationship.''

''Maybe we should dance,'' Gwen cut in, enjoying Peter's discomfort but feeling sorry for him at the same time. After all, he'd turned out pretty well considering who his mother was.

''Yes, sure.'' Peter was out of his chair in an instant and helping Gwen get to her feet.

''How about a turn around the floor?'' Jess smiled at Mary Beth and offered her his hand.

''I'd enjoy that,'' she accepted.

As the four of them reached the dance floor, the band began a slow two-step. Unlike when Jess had held her, Gwen experienced no reaction to Peter's touch. His hands simply felt heavy and nondescript and she was glad when the music stopped.

After a few more dances, Peter suggested they switch partners for a dance.

Stepping onto the dance floor, Gwen waited expectantly for Jess to hold her. When he did, her body ached to move closer to him. Every fiber of her being seemed alive with an extra energy it had never had before.

He leaned closer and whispered in her ear. ''I think our little ploy is working very well.''

His warm breath played havoc with her senses. When she tried to respond, she had to concentrate just to get out an intelligible ''It would seem so.''

''Maybe I really should let you find me a wife.''

This time when he whispered, his lips brushed against her ear, and she was barely able to swallow back a strangled moan of pleasure. "I'm sure you can find one on your own."

"But what if I find her and can't win her?"

The way he was making her feel convinced Gwen he'd have no trouble winning the woman of his dreams. "I'm sure you'll be able to win her."

"How about you?"

She frowned in confusion. "How about me what?"

"Could I win you?"

Deep within her a *yes* resounded, but it never issued. He couldn't possibly be really interested in her. He was just making small talk. "Whether you could win me or not is irrelevant. I'm not in the market for a husband."

His hand on her waist moved in a small gentle caressing motion and her blood raced. Again he leaned close. This time, his lips seemed to brush her neck when he spoke. "Your pulse is beating rapidly and your body is softening under my touch. Come on, admit it. In spite of all my rough corners, you're attracted to me."

The thought that he could honestly want her to be attracted to him…that he might consider her for a wife played through her mind. *No.* Not with her family history. More likely, she'd become a challenge his ego couldn't resist. And if she gave in, he'd regret it and she'd end up like her mother, used and not wanted any longer. Gwen gathered every ounce of resolve she had left to make her voice come out nonchalantly. "I'll admit, you're an attractive man, but that's as far as it goes."

He frowned, clearly dissatisfied with her response, and they finished the dance in silence.

For the next couple of hours, the quartet conversed in a friendly manner between dances, switching partners occasionally. All the while, Gwen could feel Wanda's gaze hard on her, but that wasn't what bothered her. What bothered her was how envious she was growing of Mary Beth. The woman had a man so in love with her he was miserable thinking he might have lost her.

And for the first time in her life, Gwen wished someone felt that way about her.

"Excuse me." Peter broke into Gwen's thoughts. He nodded toward his mother and Gwen saw Wanda motioning for her son to come speak with her.

"Wanda has smiled very nicely at me a few times tonight and she made a point of complimenting me on my dress," Mary Beth said as Peter left them. "It would seem that Gwen's plan may have worked."

"I think so," Jess replied. To Gwen, he added, "I'd say that in this case, you've proved to be an excellent matchmaker."

Gwen nodded her agreement, but her mind wasn't on Mary Beth and Peter. It was on her and Jess. She couldn't stop from visualizing herself as the right woman for him. *You'll get hurt thinking thoughts like that,* she warned herself.

When Peter returned, he took Gwen out onto the dance floor. "My mother has rethought her opinion of Mary Beth and is now strongly encouraging me to court her."

"I'm happy for you," Gwen said sincerely.

Peter glanced anxiously toward Jess and the object

of his affections. They were laughing as if they had just shared a very private joke. "I'm worried that I might be too late."

"As long as she doesn't have a ring on her finger, it's never too late," Gwen replied encouragingly.

Peter nodded. "You're right. I won't give her up without a fight."

Gwen stood leaning against a tree on the outer circle of the picnic area. It was after midnight. The band had finished packing up and those who had stayed to clean up were heading to their cars. She looked for Peter but didn't see him.

"Lost your date?"

She glanced to her left to see Jess approaching. Her heart skipped a couple of beats at the mere sight of him. The sooner she got out of town…no…the sooner she got out of the state, the better. "It would seem so. But I'm sure he'll show up sooner or later."

"The last time I saw him, he was with my date and they were heading toward the river."

"Oh."

"Mary Beth finally told him that she still loves him. And I told them that I'd get you home."

Wishing she had driven herself, Gwen straightened. *Just keep your distance from him and you'll be fine.* "It's been an interesting night."

Suddenly, unexpectedly, Gwen felt herself being lifted into two strong arms. Fighting down the intoxicating rush of heat sweeping through her, she stared at Jess in astonishment. "What…?"

"The ground is uneven and, as your very good friend, I don't want to take a chance on you tripping and falling in the dark."

"I'm sure I'll be fine." She could barely think. All she knew was that remaining cradled in his arms was dangerous. "Please, put me down."

"Nope. I'm not taking a chance on you injuring yourself."

"So you'd rather trip and fall so that we both go down together?" She sounded surprisingly in control, she thought, considering the way her body felt—as if at any moment it might spontaneously ignite.

"Mmm. Now that does sound like fun...us going down on the ground together."

He was clearly flirting with her. Erotic visions filled her mind and the desire to have him kiss her was close to overwhelming. Her little voice fought to keep her mind rational. *He's not serious. You wore a seductive dress and, like the virile male he is, he's reacting to it.* Abruptly, the inner strength she'd spent so many years nurturing came to her aid. As much as her body craved his and as tempted as she was to give in to that craving, she would not allow herself to follow in her mother's footsteps. "I insist that you put me down," she ordered stiffly.

Jess stopped, studied her quietly for a long moment, then obeyed, setting her gently on the ground.

Mentally she patted herself on the back. That he'd released her so easily gave proof that she'd read him correctly and that he'd recognized the folly of any intimacy between them. Grateful her legs remained sturdy enough to hold her, Gwen shook her head at him as they continued on to the car.

They were well on their way back to the ranch when Jess broke the silence between them. "I'm not a man who rushes into something without giving it a lot of thought. And having given the matter of you and me a great deal of my time lately, I've reached the conclusion that you're just about the right heftiness. No, not just about. You are the right heftiness."

Gwen frowned at him in confusion. "The right heftiness?"

"You're not too skinny and not too heavy. I'd say you were the perfect weight for a man my size," he elaborated, his voice businesslike.

"The perfect weight for a man your size?" *What was he up to?* His words stirred a fire deep inside while his tone was that of a man getting ready to suggest a deal. *No, deals!* she told herself firmly.

Keeping his eyes on the road, Jess continued. "Even better, you've got curves in all the right places and I'm confident they're just the right size for my hands."

With every fiber of her being, Gwen wanted to test his affirmations. "I'm not in the market for a one-night stand or even an affair," she said firmly, this statement meant even more for her own ears than for his. "I want you to take me home. To my home, not yours."

"Nope." Jess kept driving. "In spite of your protests, I'm going to have to marry you."

Marry her? He'd said he was going to marry her. *This can't be real. There has to be a catch,* her inner voice warned near panic. "Were you drinking moonshine at the picnic?"

"Nope." He slowed the car and frowned at her thoughtfully. "'Course I could be a little premature in my decision. There is one thing I haven't checked out yet."

Gwen realized that he'd brought the car to a halt. Her panic grew, but it wasn't him she was afraid of. It was herself. In the cold light of dawn, she was certain, he would regret even mentioning the words *marriage* and her name in the same sentence. But tonight, under the stars, she might weaken and give herself to him with the hope that they could have a future together.

Coming around to her side of the car, he opened the door and held out a hand. "I need you to step out here with me."

Gwen pushed herself deeper into her seat. "I'll just sit here and wait until you've come to your senses."

Reaching across her, Jess unfastened her seat belt. "I can't get the full effect with you sitting down."

His hands sent sparks coursing through her body wherever they brushed against her as he eased the seat belt off. "I never thought I'd be saying this to a Logan, but I think you've flipped out."

He gave her a patronizing look. "I'm not nuts and I'm not going to hurt you. I'm merely going to kiss you."

Kiss her? "No." The word blurted out. It was hard enough resisting him when they weren't even touching. There was no telling what a kiss might do.

"Yes. I promise it won't be painful and I'll be a gentleman at all times."

Gwen shoved herself farther back in the seat.

"Now come on. Don't be a coward." He took hold of her hands and gently coaxed her to come out of the car.

The feel of his skin against hers destroyed Gwen's resolve. All the time telling herself that she'd regret this, she allowed herself to be helped out onto the road side.

The night seemed to wrap them in a blanket of stars. And the quiet made her feel as if they were the only two people alive. Her mind ordered her legs to run, but instead she stood there, barely able to breathe, waiting for whatever was going to happen next.

Slowly, Jess drew her toward him, lowering his face to hers. When their lips met, Gwen's entire body ignited. She couldn't think beyond the delicious taste of him. Her mind reeled as he drew her hard against him and she hungered for a much more intimate contact. This was exactly the kind of reaction to a man that had led her mother down a path of destruction, her inner mind screamed at her. *And I can understand why she kept going back down that path,* she replied, her shields shattered and her resolve gone.

Just when she thought she might actually swoon from the physical effect the kiss was having on her, Gwen felt herself being released.

"Yup. I figured you'd taste as good as you look and you do," Jess announced.

"You do, too," Gwen heard herself admitting in a voice barely above a whisper.

Jess grinned and motioned for her to get back into the car.

When they were again on the road, he said, "We'll get a license Monday. There's a seventy-two hour wait. So we'll have the wedding on Friday."

"Wedding? Friday?" Gwen's jaw firmed. "You can't really mean it." A sudden thought came to mind. "Are you doing this to get back at your great-grandmother? Prove to her how far afoul her little scheme could go?"

Jess frowned at her. "Do you honestly believe I'm that kind of man. That I'd marry you just to prove my great-grandmother shouldn't have tried to mess with my life."

"Well, no. That would be stupid and you're not stupid.'' She continued to regard him narrowly. ''But I'm not sure you're entirely sane, either.''

''I suppose you could be right. I'm in love and they say that love can make a person a little crazy.''

She stared at him in disbelief. This was like a fairy tale. She had to be dreaming. ''Love? Me?''

He again brought the car to a stop on the side of the road. ''I love you and you need me. So we're getting married.''

''I don't *need* anyone.'' The statement was out before she'd even realized the words had formed. It was a knee-jerk reaction...another of the mantras she'd practiced during the years, saying it over and over to herself until it was imprinted on her mind.

He reached over and closed his large, strong, work-callused hand around hers. ''Yes, you do. You need me because I can teach you that love is real, strong and unbreakable. It's not some fragile thing that shatters as easily as glass...something that is here one minute and gone the next.''

Years of pent-up tears welled in her eyes. ''I know that, but I don't trust real love to ever find me.''

''You can trust me.'' Jess cupped her face gently in his hands and kissed her again.

When he released her Gwen sank back in her seat, all resistance gone. ''I hope so,'' she murmured.

He traced the line of her jaw with his finger. ''I promise.''

Gwen wondered if the men in her mother's life had said the same thing. She looked toward Jess as he again pulled out onto the road. Jess Logan wasn't anything like the men her mother had associated with. So maybe...

As they drove through the starlit night, a battle raged

within her. A part of her wanted to cry with joy that she'd found the love Henry had wanted for her. Another part kept warning her that she could get hurt just like her mother had been hurt. Another part envisioned her walking down the aisle with Jess and excitement flowed through her. While another part strongly suggested she pack a bag and run for the hills without looking back.

"A penny for your thoughts." Jess's voice broke the silence between them.

"They're too jumbled. Even I can't sort them out," she replied.

"I hope none of them deal with you running away." He glanced toward her. "'Cause I'd have to come looking for you. We Logan men are till-death-do-us-part kind of men once we fall in love."

A resounding *Wow* echoed in her head and a thrill raced through her. *Every man your mother ever took up with claimed that they loved her,* her little voice reminded her. She chose to ignore it. She loved Jess Logan. And this one time she was going to follow Henry's advice and take a chance. "I'll stick around." The words came out with firm resolve and she saw the corner of Jess's mouth curve into a smile.

But a while later as they mounted the porch steps and prepared to enter the house, Gwen stopped. Her love for Jess was too strong to take a chance on hurting him. The words cut like a knife, but she forced herself to say them. "There is one condition."

Jess looked at her and frowned. "There are no conditions. You have given me your word and I'm holding you to it."

She swallowed down the lump in her throat. "I can

only marry you if your family approves. You're too close to them and I won't come between you.''

Jess's hands closed around her shoulders. ''You're not getting out of marrying me. I've made up my mind.''

''I wouldn't try arguing with him,'' an elderly voice sounded from the darkened hall beyond the screened door. ''He's always been the most stubborn of the lot and that's saying a lot when you're talking about the Logan men.'' Morning Hawk, smiling widely, stepped out onto the porch. ''I've always thought the two of you would be a good match. I just couldn't quite figure out how to convince either of you of that. So I decided to put you together under the same roof and hope you were both bright enough to find out that you belong together.''

Jess grinned at his grandmother. ''Morning Hawk, the matchmaker. Wait until the rest of the family hears about this.''

Five months later, Gwen sat in the kitchen of the new house Jess had had built for them on the other side of the corrals from the original ranchhouse where his mother, grandmother and great-grandmother resided.

His family had been as surprised as she was about the marriage, but they hadn't objected. Apparently Morning Hawk's approval was all that was needed to make her a welcomed member of the family. Jess's mother and grandmother had insisted on having the ceremony at the ranch and had flown home to be there for the occasion. His brothers and their wives had also attended and all had treated her well.

Still, an uncertainty had pervaded Gwen when she and Jess had exchanged vows. No matter how hard she tried, she couldn't quell the ingrained fear that she'd inherited her mother's inability to hold on to a man's love. And as many times as she assured herself that Jess had staying power and could be trusted to stand by her, the doubt lingered.

Now, as she sat at her kitchen table, tears rolled down her cheeks.

She and Jess had had their first argument. Well, actually, not an argument. She'd woken up grouchy. She wasn't certain why. Lately, she'd been feeling a little out of sorts...her stomach was queazy and she was overly emotional. So this morning, she'd fussed at him about some things that he'd done lately that had gotten on her nerves. They weren't important things. In fact, it had been dumb of her to even let them bother her. But she had and she'd nagged him about them.

He'd simply frowned at her as if he thought she'd suddenly gone insane, then apologized gruffly and left without breakfast.

She'd thrown up in the sink, then sat down and cried. Every man her mother had loved had walked out on her for even less of a transgression.

"But I had to speed the process up with my display of foul temper." She moaned the kind of moan a child issues when it feels lost and lonely. "I tried so hard to be the perfect wife."

The sound of footsteps on the back porch caused her to straighten and brush the tears away.

"You feeling better now?" Jess asked, entering and pouring himself a cup of coffee.

"I...uh..." She stumbled around for words but was too scared to say anything.

He turned to her. "I'm sorry if I've been doing

things that upset you. Guess I have some adjustments to make.''

She stared at him in shock. "You're not leaving?" she managed to choke out after a long moment.

He smiled and shook his head. "Now why would I do something like that?"

A fresh flood of tears welled in her eyes. "I thought I'd run you off."

"It'll take a lot more than a little bit of fussing to run me off." Approaching the table, he knelt in front of her chair. "Truth is, I've been wondering where the woman I married has been. Until today, you haven't said a single critical word to me." He grinned the mischievous grin he used when he was teasing her. "Not that I'm not close to perfect."

Gwen hoped she was hearing him right…he wasn't angry with her and he was staying…but she was still too afraid to believe it.

His expression became serious. "Look, we're going to have arguments, some a lot more intense than what happened in here this morning. I've been expecting them. You're a strong woman. Truth is, you've been a lot more passive than I thought you'd be. Then this morning when you sort of exploded with that list of things that were eating at you, I figured you'd finally begun to believe I really loved you and you could be yourself. I also figured the best thing for me to do was to leave for a bit, let you cool down and then we'd talk." A hint of apprehension shadowed his features. "There were an awful lot of little things that have been eating at you and I'm not sure I can correct them overnight."

"I don't expect you to be perfect," she returned shakily. "And I was way overly critical." The tears spilled over the rims of her eyes and flowed down her cheeks. "I don't know what happened. I've just been so on edge lately."

"Anyone would get overly stressed trying to be something they're not. You've been trying to be a doormat. That's not in your character." He took her hands in his. "You're my woman, Gwen. A few harsh words aren't going to change the way I feel about you."

Gwen suddenly felt the nausea bubbling up once more. "I'm going to be sick," she said, pushing her chair back, breaking free from his hold, rising and heading to the sink again.

"Thank goodness for garbage disposals," she murmured a few minutes later as she cleaned the sink and splashed cold water on her face.

Jess was standing at the counter studying her narrowly. "I'm thinking that your edginess could be caused by something more than you merely trying to be something you're not."

She looked at him in confusion.

"Seems to me like you're a little late this month."

Gwen's gaze shot to the calendar on the wall. She'd been so strung out lately, she hadn't realized she was two weeks late. "I am." Understanding showed on her face. "And being pregnant would explain the nausea I've had for the past couple of mornings."

In the next instant, Jess had scooped her up in his arms. "Morning Hawk's going to be ecstatic. Not only has she seen me wed, but she's going to be around to see our children," he said, grinning down at Gwen with a face that glowed with love.

She smiled up at him. "I love you, Jess Logan."

His expression turned serious. "It's about time you said that."

She frowned at him. "I have."

"Nope. I knew you did. But you never actually said the words."

It occurred to Gwen that deep within a tiny residue of self-protection had kept her from saying those words to him. But now that was gone. She trusted her husband with all her heart and finally, after a lifetime of believing it would never happen to her, she accepted the fact that she had found everlasting love. "I love you. I love you. I love you," she said happily.

With a happy grin, he kissed her.

* * * * *

If you enjoyed what you just read,
then we've got an offer you can't resist!

Take 2 bestselling love stories FREE!
Plus get a FREE surprise gift!

Clip this page and mail it to Silhouette Reader Service™

IN U.S.A.	IN CANADA
3010 Walden Ave.	P.O. Box 609
P.O. Box 1867	Fort Erie, Ontario
Buffalo, N.Y. 14240-1867	L2A 5X3

YES! Please send me 2 free Silhouette Romance® novels and my free surprise gift. After receiving them, if I don't wish to receive anymore, I can return the shipping statement marked cancel. If I don't cancel, I will receive 6 brand-new novels every month, before they're available in stores! In the U.S.A., bill me at the bargain price of $3.34 plus 25¢ shipping and handling per book and applicable sales tax, if any*. In Canada, bill me at the bargain price of $3.80 plus 25¢ shipping and handling per book and applicable taxes**. That's the complete price and a savings of at least 10% off the cover prices—what a great deal! I understand that accepting the 2 free books and gift places me under no obligation ever to buy any books. I can always return a shipment and cancel at any time. Even if I never buy another book from Silhouette, the 2 free books and gift are mine to keep forever.

215 SDN DNUM
315 SDN DNUN

Name	(PLEASE PRINT)	
Address	Apt.#	
City	State/Prov.	Zip/Postal Code

* Terms and prices subject to change without notice. Sales tax applicable in N.Y.
** Canadian residents will be charged applicable provincial taxes and GST.
All orders subject to approval. Offer limited to one per household and not valid to current Silhouette Romance® subscribers.
® are registered trademarks of Harlequin Books S.A., used under license.

SROM02   ©1998 Harlequin Enterprises Limited

SILHOUETTE Romance

COMING NEXT MONTH

SRCNM0403